MOORS

Jan Michael, born outside Wigglesworth in the Yorkshire Dales, has lived much of her life abroad, eventually returning to live and work in Settle where this story is set. She has had thirteen books published, several of which are for children. Many have been translated, all into Dutch, others variously into German, Japanese, Italian, Polish and Danish; two were turned into operas. Her latest children's book *Leaving Home* was published in the U.K., the U.S.A. and the Netherlands where it won two prestigious prizes, the Silver Slate Pencil for best translated fiction, and the Dutch IBBY prize.

Praise for *Hill of Darkness* by the same author:
　'[An] atmospheric, unusual novel.' *Guardian*
　Just Joshua:
　'A heart-warming book that retains its spell even when you have finished reading it.' *De Morgen,* Belgium
　Leaving Home:
　'Vivid descriptions of place, character, mood and atmosphere…. The ending is warm and satisfying.' *School Librarian*
　'I enjoyed the book from start to finish. There was nothing I disliked.' *Evening Echo,* Ireland (review by twelve-year-old)

Also by Jan Michael

Hill of Darkness
Flying Crooked
Just Joshua
The Rock Boy
Leaving Home

Moorside Boy

jan michael

G
Gabriel Press

First published in Great Britain in 2013
by Gabriel Press
9 Lower Croft Street, Settle, North Yorkshire BD24 9HH
www.jan-michael.co.uk

All rights reserved. No part of this publication may be reproduced, stored in a retrieval system, or transmitted in any form or by any means, electronic, mechanical, photocopying, recording or otherwise without the written permission of the publisher

Copyright © 2013 Jan Michael

The right of Jan Michael to be identified as the author of this work has been asserted by her in accordance with the Copyright, Designs and Patents Act, 1988

British Library Cataloguing in Publication Data available
ISBN 978-0-9576533-0-6

Printed and bound in Great Britain by
Lamberts Print & Design
2 Station Road, Settle, North Yorkshire BD24 9AA

For
Alice and Rocco
Louis and Theadora

This is almost a true story.

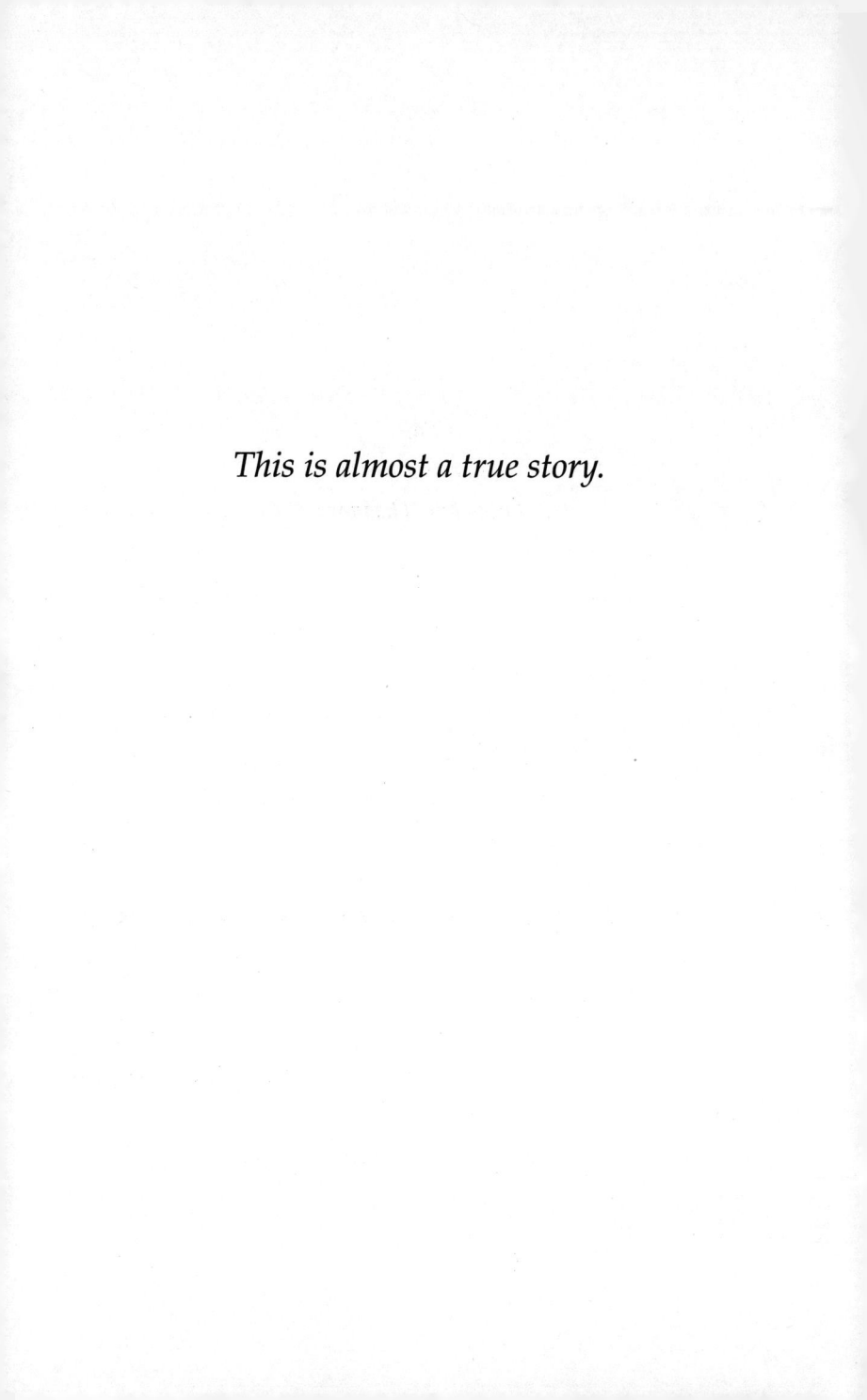

He'd said I was no charmer.

I was all right, wasn't I? I was like any other boy, more or less, wasn't I? Reddish hair, two ears, pointy chin, two eyes.

But I suppose my eyes were piercing, the way they looked back at me in the mirror, bright and blue. My reflection stuck a tongue out at me.

I stared. My tongue was in my mouth. I hadn't stuck it out.

My reflection laughed at me.

But I wasn't laughing. I turned around to check that there was no one but me in the room, even though it felt daft, even though I knew there wasn't.

The reflection raised a hand. His hair was so dark it was almost black. But mine was red. His neck was hidden under a high collar. It looked woollen and scratchy.

I pushed my hands in my pockets.

The boy in the mirror beckoned. His blue eyes bored into mine.

I took out one hand. Slowly, I raised it and pressed it to the glass.

One

If only he hadn't taken me to school. That's when things really began to go wrong.

'Percival Benjamin Waugh,' Mum's friend said, introducing me. His voice rang out in the quiet classroom. Everyone else was already there and seated.

My mouth fell open. Why did he say all my names? And why so loudly, so that the whole class could hear? Soon after Mum had met her friend, my village school back home at Wrath had closed. 'That's a bit of luck,' he'd said, 'another reason for moving in with me; Seggleswick's got a good school,' and we'd come to his house in this market town, a week after September term had begun. 'I'll take him to school,' he said that morning, 'my town, my privilege.'

'Percival Benjamin?' the teacher repeated, but Mum's friend had already turned on his heel and left.

Behind me the class was choking with laughter. My face was getting hot. I knew I was turning red.

The teacher came away from the whiteboard. 'Quiet, you lot!' Even when he stooped down like a question mark, he was tall. 'That's a mouthful! What do they call you at home?' he asked.

'Percy.'

'Right-o,' he said. His eyes were warm; they looked like spider's webs at the corner there were that many crinkles.

'How do you spell your surname?'

'W-a-u-g-h,' I answered. 'Waugh.'

'Ah. Round here we say "wuff" rather than "war".'

That made it worse. 'Wuff! wuff!' someone barked behind me. Others joined in.

The teacher stared over my head at the class. The barking stopped.

'My name is Mr Magnus. Welcome.' He tugged at his waistcoat. It was as green as my bright marker pen and was covered in red dots. 'There's a place for you at that table.' He pointed to his right. 'Daniel, will you show Percy the ropes, please.'

Daniel pushed a chair out from the table and I slid in.

At break, everyone charged out. 'Come on,' Daniel said, but I felt shy so I was slow and he was gone.

'Hey, you!' a voice shouted when I did get outside.

I turned. A group of girls were staring at me.

'What's your name again?'

'Percy.'

'It's not: it's Percival.' A girl giggled. 'And what about your other names?'

'Percival Benjamin,' another sniggered.

They doubled up laughing.

I smiled, trying not to look as if I cared, and went over and stood with my back to the fence, hoping to spot Daniel.

The teacher on duty came over. 'Why don't you go and play football with the others? You look pretty strong and wiry. Fast, are you? Do you like being on wing? Hey, you lot.' She strode over to a group of boys. 'Let- what's your name?'

'Percy.'

'Let Percy in to play with you.' She nudged me forward.

'Here, Percival Benjamin!' One lad swerved towards me and ran away again with the ball. Daniel saw me and kicked a curving ball at me. I only went and missed it!

'Wuff! Wuff!' they barked.

It wasn't a good start.

'Why've I got those names!' I shouted as I ran into Mum's friend's house after school. Uncle Ian, Mum asked me to call him now we were here. But he wasn't my uncle, so I wouldn't. I might have done. I hadn't minded him at first when he'd come to ours, in Wrath. He'd put a net up in our garden, even if he did say it was more like a field than a garden, and we'd shot goals. Sometimes Mum had been in goal – she was so hopeless he'd laughed at her like I had. It was fun. Mum used to sing a lot just after he'd gone, and be all dreamy. He looked all right, almost like a movie star with that dark hair and sharp jaw. Sometimes I'd lie in bed imagining he could be my dad. Now we were here I wasn't so sure.

Look at him now, wincing, staring at my trainers on his shiny floor. 'Percy, please. Go back and take off your shoes. You know the rules of the house.'

I ignored him. Saying my names loudly this morning so the whole class could hear! 'Why have I, Mum?'

'Shoes, first, love.'

I stomped back to the front door. I kicked my trainers off on top of the shoes lined up neatly by the door. Mum was right behind me, and we hugged. Her hair didn't tickle my face as usual; she'd pulled it off her face and piled it up on top. 'Do you like it?' she asked when she saw me looking. 'Ian says it's elegant.' I followed her back into the sitting part of the huge downstairs room, perched on the arm of her chair, and buried my nose in her neck. Mum always smelled good, like oranges and honey.

'I've made us chocolate cake for tea,' she said.

'Your favourite,' he chipped in, 'since it was your first day at a new school. Percy, please don't sit on that arm. You'll ruin the chair.'

I moved to the small table at Mum's side. He cleared his throat, *grrhum*.

I suppose I wasn't to sit there either. I sat on the floor.

'There's no need to sit on the floor,' he said. 'There are plenty of chairs.'

Maybe, but they were right over on the other side of the room, and I wanted to be close to Mum, to talk to her.

'Why don't we have our tea now,' Mum said quickly. 'I've got sausages, the ones you like, then you can tell us about school,' she went on. 'I'll go and get on with cooking.'

'You,' he said, stopping me as I was about to follow. 'Go and wash your hands and comb your hair first.'

It was one thing after another: shoes off, hands, hair. It was no good appealing to Mum. She said it was good for me to have rules, that I'd lived too long without them and that her Ian knew what was what. She said I was 'anarchic' and that I couldn't be anarchic for ever. So I went to the downstairs loo and turned on the tap, ran my fingers under it and wiped them on my sleeves. Then I smoothed down my hair, or tried to, except that it sprang back up. I stuck out my tongue at the mirror, then kicked the door shut behind me as I hurried to the kitchen.

'We don't slam doors in this house. We shut them quietly.'

Mum glanced at him and then at me.

'Sorry,' I muttered.

'Fair enough,' he said.

'Good lad.' Mum ruffled my hair as I passed her on my way to the kitchen table. It was square and solid and you had to sit on high stools. It was big enough for at least half my class to sit round. Or lots of his friends - if he had any; I hadn't met them yet.

'Why did you call me- '

'Here.' He hooked one foot round a stool and pushed it towards me.

I sat.

'Now. What was it that you wanted to ask your mother?'

I turned my back on him. 'Mum, why did you call me Percival?' I burst out. 'It's so long. And Benjamin, too. They're horrible.'

'Oh! I didn't know you thought that.' She came and sat down, too. Next to him.

'No one's called them out loud before. He did,' I glared at him, 'in front of the whole class.'

She looked startled. 'Did you?' she asked him.

'Yes, of course. They're his names, aren't they? I thought it was the correct form. I'm sorry if I was out of order. Well, my darling, why did you?' *Grrghum*, he cleared his throat. 'We want to know, don't we, young man?' He leaned over and dug me in the ribs.

I shifted out of reach.

'Take Percival, for starters,' he went on. 'Knight of the Round Table. I mean,' he pointed at me, 'look at him. What a scruff! Look at your collar, half in, half out. And is that mud on the cuff of your school sweater? I can't quite imagine Sir Percival looking like that!' He brayed with laughter, *hoik, hoik,* just like a donkey. 'It is a bit of an unfortunate name, isn't it. I'm on Percy's side here. Mind, not that Percy's much better, is it. Point Percy at the porcelain. You know what Percy means there, don't you, eh?'

I felt hot and knew I was blushing again. I couldn't help it with my red hair.

'Ian!' Mum remonstrated. 'I don't think that's very funny. Did they tease you, love?'

I nodded.

'Oh, numkin. Listen, there's nothing wrong with Percy, nothing at all. Percival was your father's name. You know that.'

'That doesn't mean you had to call me it! You could have called me Tom, or John, something normal.'

'I thought your father would be pleased. At the time. When you were born, he was away in France, so I had to name you and register you on my own.'

'But he didn't come back, did he?'

'Didn't he?' her friend echoed.

She turned, including him. 'Yes, he did,' she said in a flat voice. 'When he came to pick up his things and told me he was leaving. Six months later I had a letter from a woman in France saying he'd been in a car crash, and he'd died.' Her mouth twisted.

'So whatever you called me, he wouldn't have cared.' I didn't want to let it go.

'I did give you another name, one all of your own. I called you Benjamin. Come on, pet, tell us about school. Did you make friends?'

I shrugged. 'And why've I got such a silly last name? They're calling me Wuff.'

'Are they? Well, I can't help your surname,' she said sharpish. 'Anyway, Wuff's how your grandfather pronounced it when he was alive.'

'You never said,' I said grumpily. I pushed aside my plate and reached for the cake.

'Finish your sausages first. Savoury, then sweet. Your mother's made your favourite cake, too. What do you say?'

'Thank you. But I don't need you to tell me what to say to Mum!'

'Percy!' It was Mum. 'What is the matter with you?'

What was the matter with *me*? What was the matter with *him*, the way he kept butting in.

I picked up my knife and fork and had another mouthful of sausage but I wasn't hungry any longer. My fingers found a knot in the wood of the table and I pressed harder and harder into it. I wanted to tell Mum about school, but I wanted her on her own. And now I'd missed my chance because she was listening to him talk about his day in Pipton where he was manager at some supermarket.

At last he stopped and Mum turned to me. 'Come on, pet, you now.'

'Later.'

She sighed. 'Percy, if you're going to sulk, why don't you go to your room?'

He smirked, I'm sure of it. Mum was looking at me so she

didn't see.

I went. Halfway up the stairs, I turned. He was holding her and she was nestling into him, lifting her head for a kiss.

'Mum, will you come up?' I called.

'Yes, love,' she said.

So I sat on my bed and waited. Downstairs I could hear them laughing together, his *hoik hoik*, and her gurgling chuckle. I pulled on my pyjamas and got into bed. It was better in there, under my old duvet; I'd chosen it for my last birthday and it had Dr Who Tardisses on it. I reached for Woody and cuddled him while I waited.

'Oh, are you in bed already?' she said, coming into the room. 'Look, I brought you some cake. Will you have it now, while you tell me how it was at school?'

I was still cross and miserable so I shook my head. 'Mum, he says silly things.'

'He doesn't mean them to be silly. Look at it from his point of view, numkin. He's not used to having a lad about the place. He's never had to share this house before.'

'I didn't ask him to.'

'No, I know. But I did. And I want you to try harder to get on. You got on all right before. Finished?' She took the plate from me. She tucked my duvet all round me and hugged me in a bundle, the way I liked. 'I'm sorry if it's been a rotten day for you. Tomorrow will be better, you'll see.' She kissed me. 'And Ian is doing what he can; he only wants the best for you; he took you to school, didn't he.'

'Wish he hadn't,' I mumbled into the pillow.

'Goodnight, numkin.' She waited, in case I answered, but I didn't.

When she'd gone, I was sorry. There was this huge lump in my chest; it crept up into my throat and higher, and I started to cry. I'd kind of wanted to come here to live; it'd felt like an adventure. He'd liked our place in Wrath, he'd played with me, he'd been all right. But from the moment we'd got here, things became different, and now he'd spoilt school, too. I'd made no friends because of the way he'd called out my names. If it had just been Mum and me I'd have told her all about the day, and she'd have made it feel better. But he was in the way. Tears gushed out of my eyes and on to Woody who got wetter and wetter. In the end I got out of bed and lay on the floor with my ear to the floorboard, listening to the rise and fall of their voices, and their laughter, and then how their voices dropped to a murmur. I was almost asleep on the floor when I heard the back door being shut and the rasp of the key turning, the click, click of windows being closed. Then the front door was opened and shut below. He always did that before locking it and putting the key away. Finally, the rattle of a bolt being drawn shut. He locked and shut everything. We'd not bothered locking in Wrath.

I jumped into bed as two lots of footsteps sounded on the stairs. My door opened, throwing a triangle of light on the floor.

'Percy?' said his voice. 'Are you still awake?'

I clutched Woody tightly, pretending to be asleep.

'Goodnight, love,' Mum said.

The door closed.

I scrunched the duvet round my shoulders and knelt at the end of the bed to look out of the window. Far over to the right I could make out the top of the church tower, and a corner of the graveyard, and the gravestones shining in the moonlight. I gazed at them till my eyelids drooped and my head sank on to the window sill.

There was the smell of cut grass in my nose and the song of a blackbird in my ears, and in my dream I was walking through the flower meadow that sloped down from our cottage in Wrath. The meadow stretched on and on, down and down, towards a stream. As I reached the stream a wall appeared. I stepped over it easily. Behind me it grew tall and thick. In front of me graves glowed the colour of honey in the sunshine. I lay on my back on one, and the sun warmed me, and the tombstone at my back sheltered me from the breeze. Further up sheep were grazing. It was as if I knew it from somewhere. I sank into deep sleep.

Two

'Good morning.' It was him. 'Up you get. Breakfast's on the table.'

I yawned. 'In a minute.'

'And do you think you could be civil today? Do you hear me, young man? Come on, up. Now.' He picked my bear up from the floor by an arm. Woody must have fallen out of bed in the night. 'Look, *teddy's* getting up.'

'Give me Woody!' I scrambled out of bed. Too late. He'd swung him out through the open window.

How could he! I rushed past him and down the stairs in my pyjamas and bare feet.

'Percy? Where are you going?' Mum called.

I didn't stop. I fumbled with the locks on the door, finally got into the garden, and picked up Woody and hugged him close.

'He threw Woody out,' I shouted at Mum, running back indoors and upstairs.

'It was a joke,' I heard him say. 'Can't you take a joke, young man?'

'I wish you hadn't done that.' I heard her through my open door.

'It's only a teddy bear, for heaven's sake. Isn't he too old for teddies?'

'Woody is special,' Mum said. 'Surely you can understand that.'

He muttered something. Then her voice dropped too. I thought I heard her say something like '...make it up to him.'

After breakfast, Mum walked with me on the way to school. We stopped on the footbridge where the river tumbled round a big rock in the middle and smaller ones around. How must it be for fish below in the water, plunging and darting through the gaps in the rocks to the calmer waters beyond.

Mum nudged me. I hadn't spotted the heron on the bank, one skinny leg on a stone, the other tucked up beneath him, staring at the water, still as a statue. He was waiting to stab his long beak into a fish and stop its swimming for ever. I willed him not to get one.

Mum gasped. 'Percy, look at the time!' She held her wristwatch out to me. 'You'll be late!'

I tore my eyes away from the heron, hefted my bag back on my shoulder and started to run.

'Hey! Haven't you forgotten something?'

I raced back for her kiss.

'Now go! Go! Good luck!'

I was late getting in to class, and had to race after the others to assembly.

I slid on to the bench beside Daniel. The little ones were already seated in front of us cross-legged on the floor, singing 'Op-en the book,' clap clap, 'Op-en the book,' clap clap. A man in a white gown and headdress, a woman dressed as an angel, and a guy in a helmet were acting out some Bible story.

'On your feet, P.' Everyone was standing. 'That's what I'll call you,' Daniel said under his breath.

'P?' I said. 'Why? I don't want to be called P. I mean...' everyone'd think of it as Pee. Me too.

'Yes, you do. It's easier and shorter than all those names. Less daft.'

Less daft?!

'Blow your trumpet.'

'I haven't got a trumpet.'

'So pretend. We're to blow our trumpets and march round the walls of Jericho till they fall down, dumbo.'

'What walls of Jericho?'

'Can't you see them? The ones round the man with the cardboard over his head.' Daniel snorted.

I followed him into the line that snaked round the edges of the room, and ended up joining in, tooting and blasting away with the rest of them.

'Hallelujah! They're down!' cried the man in the white robe and headdress, who was being Joshua from the Bible.

Back in the classroom, I stared down at my book. It'd be good to do that: blow a pretend trumpet and blast and shout so the man's house would topple over and we could go back to ours.

'Percy! You haven't got very far.' Mr Magnus was leaning over my chair.

The map of Holland we were supposed to be filling in came back into focus. Which dots represent the city of Amsterdam? Which Rotterdam? Name them. I needed a pencil. I reached for Louise's spare one.

'That's *mine*, Percival Benjamin!' she said sharply, getting to it first and tapping the back of my hand with it. Her nose, which was pink where her thick glasses pinched, went redder.

'I know it's yours. Can I borrow it?'

She tapped my hand again, only harder.

Mr Magnus turned back. 'Laura,' he warned. 'What did our class decide was important?'

'To be responsible, considerate, lively and clever, happy, look tidy and not be annoying,' she chanted.

'Correct,' said Mr Magnus. 'But haven't you left one out?'

Louise pursed her lips, considering. 'Friendly to all?' she said finally.

'Precisely. Percy, try again.'

'Can I borrow your pencil?'

'Yes. I would have said yes before if you'd asked and asked nicely.'

She sounded just like Mum's friend. Daniel rolled his eyes. 'Take no notice,' he said. 'Louise's like that. Aren't you, Louise?'

'Sometimes,' sniffed Louise, tossing her thin ponytail.

'Anyway, listen, you. From now on we're calling him P,' Daniel told her.

When school was over, everyone just seemed to disappear. The heron was gone, too. I waited, keeping guard, watching the river curl and froth round the rocks below, but it didn't come back. When I got to the house they were both in.

'Shoes,' Mum's friend started to say, but I'd already turned back to take them off. They were at the table, and Mum had put out crusty bread and cheese and the rest of the chocolate cake, and started to pour out tea and lemonade. There was a package there, too.

'Aren't you giving it to him then?' Mum asked.

'Here.' He slid it across the wide table, not quite looking at me.

'For me?'

'Don't look so surprised.'

'What is it?'

'Open it and see.'

I tore off the paper. 'Wow! Thanks, Mum.'

'Don't thank me. Thank Uncle Ian. It's from him. It's *very* generous of you.' She touched his hand.

'Thank you.' I couldn't stop grinning. I'd wanted a Lego technic log loader kit for ages. It had more than five hundred pieces and you could make a tractor or a crane, all sorts of things.

He looked pleased too. 'Did you know,' he said, as we ate some Mum's crusty bread, 'did you know that you should chew your food thirty-two times for optimum benefit and to avoid indigestion?'

'I thought it was forty-three,' Mum said, sounding serious. But really she was teasing him.

'No, thirty-two. We should all try.'

Mum winked at me, so we did, keeping straight faces. I gave up after eleven, had to swallow my mouthful. He was still chewing. 'How many?' I asked.

He held up all fingers. Ten. And again, twenty. He didn't stop chewing. Mum raised her eyebrows at me and grinned; she'd stopped long ago.

After tea I took the Lego to the corner where there was lots of space and spread out the pieces and read the instruction booklet, trying to decide what to make first. I lined up the pieces, getting ready to start. After an hour or so and going a bit wrong, I'd almost completed the chassis and had sorted the next pieces I'd need.

In the morning I came down early to do a bit more work on the loader before breakfast and school. The corner of the room was empty. I stared. It stayed empty, except for Mum's friend sitting nearby in an armchair, reading the paper. I ran through to the kitchen. 'Where's my Lego?'

'Ask Uncle Ian,' Mum said, and plonked a teapot on the table.

I left the kitchen and went and stood in front of him so he'd put down his paper. 'Where's my Lego?'

'Good morning, Percival,' he said quietly.

Why was he calling me Percival? He must know I hated it.

'Aren't you going to say good morning first?' he went on.

'What's happened to my log loader?'

'Good morning,' he repeated.

'Morning,' I huffed. 'What's happened to it?'

'Nothing.' He pointed. 'It's up there, on the shelf. I tidied it away.'

'But the pieces were ready for the next bit. They were all in order.'

'You can start again, can't you? The pieces haven't walked. But we can't have bits of Lego cluttering up the place. Anyone could slip on one and break a leg.'

'It was in the *corner*. It wasn't in anyone's way.'

'Subject closed, young man.' He straightened his paper till it crackled. I wished *he'd* slipped on a piece. I glared at him.

What was he like!

'Don't do that,' he said, shifting in his chair. 'Those eyes of yours! So piercing,' he muttered to himself. Then to me, 'It's rude to stare. Has no one told you that?'

I suppose by no one he meant Mum. That made me crosser. 'No.'

He gazed at me. *Gowk!* I hissed silently at him in my mind as I stared back. He didn't want me there and I didn't want to be there. I guessed he was speaking quietly so Mum couldn't hear. That's what he was, a great big cuckoo in Mum's and my nest. Gowk! That's what I'd call him. He dropped his eyes first. 'Go and have your breakfast. You're no charmer, that's for sure.'

I ate my cereal and toast quickly. I wanted to get out of there. I ran up for my school bag, almost banging my head on the mirror by the door in my haste. And stopped. He'd said I was no charmer. But I was all right, wasn't I? I was like any other boy, more or less, wasn't I? Reddish hair, two ears, pointy chin, two eyes.

But I suppose my eyes were piercing, the way they looked back at me, bright and blue. My reflection stuck a tongue out at me.

I stared. My tongue was in my mouth. I hadn't stuck it out.

My reflection laughed at me.

But I wasn't laughing. I turned around to check that there was no one but me in the room, even though it felt daft, even though I knew there wasn't.

The reflection raised a hand. His hair was so dark it was almost black. His neck was hidden under a high collar. It looked woollen and scratchy.

I pushed my hands in my pockets.

The boy in the mirror beckoned. His blue eyes bored into mine.

I took out one hand. Slowly, I raised it and pressed it to the glass.

Nothing happened.

I thought the reflection would put his hand on mine and press back. He didn't. He was gone. It felt as if a friend had left the room.

Three

Daniel was friendly enough in class. But once school was over, I was nobody. He and Tim and Harry from the next table headed off towards the centre of town. I heard them say so. I tagged along behind, as if I was going that way anyway and hoping they'd ask me to join them. They didn't exactly ask me not to, but they didn't include me either. I kicked a pebble towards Daniel thinking it'd hit his shoe and get his attention, but it hit a passing woman's ankle instead and she turned and frowned at me.

When we reached a newsagent's on the corner with me still behind, I called, all cool, 'See you later.'

They didn't hear me. I hung back for a moment, in case. Then I turned into the shop and bought a bag of fudge, then ripped the plastic bag open with my teeth as I walked across the square. I wished they had asked me to join them. I'd told Mum I didn't need her to meet me from school, but now I wished she had. I felt lonelier than I'd ever been. I knew no one here and no one knew me. I'd never felt so sorry for myself. Probably no one cared. It wasn't like Wrath with a few houses scattered in open fields and moors; here old stone buildings huddled together and came right on to ginnels and pavements, hemming me in. Above them loomed a great cliff that looked a castle ruin. All those stones must have witnessed so much over the years, over the centuries.

I wandered up the market square and leaned back against the wall of a building on the corner and took out a lump of fudge. I pushed my tongue against it till it crumbled and melted chocolate and sugar all over my teeth. I pressed back against the stone behind. It was solid, ancient. I was taking out another lump of fudge when my eyes caught: BENJAMIN WAUGH. Two of my names, engraved there in the stone! I stared at them. Benjamin Waugh. I reached out and ran my finger over the letters, B-E-. Then at the N, my finger snagged; the bottom bit of the letter was missing. It felt odd. I went on. J-A-. This time my finger seemed to stick in the groove of the A coming down, and the line blurred. The letters on either side swam in front of my eyes, making me dizzy. It was as if I was being pulled into the wall.

I tore my eyes away just as a group of women who'd been chatting nearby shimmered and dissolved; in their place a horse and cart came clopping past. 'Oy! Scallywag! Outta the way!' the carter shouted as a boy in rags and with bare feet ran out from almost under his wheels. 'Much obliged!' the carter snorted. He looked peculiar, dressed in a leather jerkin with great boots up to his knees. I stared. I could still taste fudge, at least I thought I could, but there was no plastic bag in my hand now. Besides which, I had my hands in my pockets, and wool scratched against my wrists where they rested against woollen trousers.

From a flower shop opposite wafted over a sweet smell. 'Gillyflowers,' said a voice and a woman in a white cotton cap and a long brown gown nipped in at the waist was standing in front of me, her head tilted to one side as she admired the blooms. 'Are they not bonny, our Benjamin? I have a gift for you. Mr Nelson the cobbler made it specially, at my request. How he found the time, I cannot imagine. He is a good man, that Titus Nelson. Here you are.'

I took the parcel eagerly.

'Take off the wrappings. Be careful, mind.'

I untied the string and unfolded the brown paper. Inside was a square wooden box, painted blue, with a slot on top. A money box. 'Thank you, Mother,' I heard myself say.

She smiled. 'Read what is written on it. I painted the words myself.'

They twirled in yellow against the blue of the box. 'To do good, forget not.'

'It's for you, our Benjamin. You might like to save to buy strong red flannel for the poor.'

'Like pennies from heaven?'

'That's my lad. Like pennies from heaven,' she agreed. 'Come here while I embrace you.'

My head reeled as she held me close. The world shifted. A motorbike roared past, trailing petrol fumes behind it.

My arms were stretched out into thin air. I lowered them and looked around. What had all that been about? I was Percy, standing on the corner of a square in front of a bank in a town I didn't know. Where had the woman I'd called Mother gone? There was no wooden box in my hand, only a bag of fudge. I stared at it. I shoved it in my pocket and got moving.

Mum was alone when I got back. I took a good look at her.

She was my mother all right, she really was, even if she was wearing the same boring brown jumper as the day before. 'I got some fudge. Here.' I pushed the bag in her hands as I kicked off my shoes at the door.

She knelt to put them straight before hugging me: 'Hello, love.'

That was a Mum-hug all right. I felt giddy with relief and kicked the shoes untidy once more as I followed her through.

'Is there any of that cake left?'

'No, we finished it. Until I find a job I've time on my hands. I've made a lemon drizzle one as a special treat, second day at your new school.'

Great! 'Can we take it outside? And play cards?'

'Sure, and have tea. So, how was school today?'

'OK.' I'd tell her after playing cards. I loved playing games with Mum.

'First, I've got you something.' From behind her back she produced a china sheep. It was white, with a black face; in its back was a slot. 'Ta-da! Look what I found! It's a piggy bank - except that it's a sheep not a pig. So – a sheepy bank.'

A sheepy bank! I was startled. The china was cold against my hot hand. My mind whirled. I felt sick. 'Must I save up for flannel for the poor?'

'You what? Flannels, you mean? Face flannels? Why would you want to do that? You funny love.' She stroked my cheek. 'It's for you to put away some pocket money, each week. Save it and buy something you want. Here,' she dropped in 50p, 'there's the first contribution.'

Pennies from heaven, I remembered. 'For the poor?' I needed to check.

'What poor?' She peered at me. 'Percy?'

'I had...' What?

'Are you all right?'

I shook my head, 'I'm OK.' For a split second I'd been about to tell her about the other mother. But what would I say? She'd think I was going mad. 'I'll fetch the cards,' I said.

I ran up to my room and put the sheepy bank on the windowsill, facing out. At the door I halted at the mirror again. I saw just me: my eyes that Mum said were as bright as bluebells, my freckles which were just like hers. She was Mum, I was Percy. As for what had happened before, it must have been a dream, mustn't it? Or I'd just imagined it. I raced back downstairs, repeating me, Mum, me, Mum, over and over again to myself.

She was already putting a tray down on the front doorstep. We sat each side of the tray and the sun shone on us and it all seemed less important. The lemony goo spread inside my mouth and we licked our fingers clean. 'What'll we play, beggar my neighbour or gin rummy?'

'Rummy,' I decided. I won the first round, and the second. 'Seventy-eight, forty to me!' I passed her the pack. 'Your deal.'

She was shuffling when her hand stopped. A silver car was drawing up. She put down the cards.

'Mu-um, deal.'

But she was already on her feet and going to meet the gowk. They hugged each other.

'I don't think this is quite the thing,' he said, giving me a scratchy smile over her head. 'What will the neighbours say, seeing you out here like this?'

I didn't think any neighbours were watching. 'Why does it

matter? We played cards outside in Wrath.'

'There's no need to sit on the doorstep when we've got perfectly good garden chairs, is there.'

That was daft. In Wrath there hadn't been a doorstep, so how could we have played on it? 'Come, let's go inside,' he went on. 'We can slide open the glass wall if you want fresh air.'

He tried to take my arm, too, but I moved away and he dropped it, looking silly.

In Wrath we'd walked straight out on to grass which Mum let grow tall, and there'd been flowers scattered in it like the farmer's hay meadow, with flashes of white and yellow, blue and purple and pink. Here was a flowerbed with flowers in a row like soldiers at the side of a smooth lawn. Which was why, he'd explained when we got here, we couldn't put up my goalposts and kick a ball around.

'Bring the cards, we'll finish the game inside,' Mum said.

I trailed indoors behind them, forgotten. Mum and he were talking and I knew we wouldn't finish the game. I didn't much feel like Lego either; he'd only clear it away. Upstairs in my room, I looked around. Not that there was much to see. When we moved Mum had got all enthusiastic about 'decluttering'. Now that we were here in his house with bare surfaces, or else one jug on a glass shelf here, a pot alone on a stone shelf there, I guessed the decluttering had been his idea. There were a couple of my books and Woody, and my duvet cover. Not much else. A bed, a chair, a shelf, cupboard, small rug, a window which only opened at the top, a door. No, two doors. One led outside. 'It's not to be used,' he'd said. 'The steps outside are lethal.'

I knelt on my bed and opened the top window as far as I could and stuck my head out to look at the steps. They didn't look dangerous to me. I scrambled off the bed and examined the door. It was bolted, top and bottom, and there was a keyhole. Carefully I wiggled open the top bolt, and the bottom. Then I tried the handle. The door wouldn't open. It was locked. I bolted it again.

I went back downstairs. He was cooking. I picked up the cards and held them up to Mum to see, but it was no good, she wasn't playing, she was in the middle of telling him about an interview for a job she hadn't got. I slumped in the leather chair in the corner, wishing for our old sofa that dipped at one end to form a hollow just the right size to curl up in. Here it was tight lines and glass and steel and everything in its place. 'It gives a sense of space and freedom,' he'd said. I thought we were freer before.

Four

'Right, "The Highwayman". I'd like you to storyboard the poem.' Mr Magnus dangled the book of poetry from his hand. 'If you were going to tell someone the story, what episodes would you put in? Tell it in your own words. First, a few points. The highwayman himself, with his claret-coloured velvet coat and lace at his wrists and throat and - yes, do you want to say something, Harry?'

'And a c-cocked hat and d-d-doeskin breeches.'

'Good. We shall rely upon you to furnish us with more detail. Now then, what do you think about the highwayman - a goodie or a baddie? Yes, Louise?'

'A baddie,' Louise called out.

'Yes. He's a thief, isn't he? Does anyone here have a different opinion, goodie or baddie?'

'A bit of both.'

'Good, Daniel, O fount of all wisdom. Why does Daniel think he's a bit of a goodie too? Yes, Tracey.'

'Because he comes back for Bess, and he's brave.'

'He's brave and he comes back for Bess, the innkeeper's black-eyed daughter. Fair point.'

'What's he want to smell her hair for?' asked Kyle. 'That's

disgusting.'

'Why would he want to smell her hair? It's a sloppy romantic thing, yeh. You'll understand later. You can leave out the slushy bit if you want, Kyle.'

'Mr Magnus?'

'Yes, Percy. Hand up first, please.'

'Is he a ghost?'

'I think so, yes. Don't you? But let's not go there. Right, everyone, find a double-page spread and storyboard the poem. Think of the feel, the mood, the ambience. Then break up the story into six ideas. Go into as much detail as you can, so long as it's good.'

'Can we draw a picture?'

'You probably can, Louise. May you? Yes, you may, so long as you've done the writing first. Go.'

'Daniel.' I nudged him. 'Do you know about ghosts? Do you believe in them?'

'Dunno.'

'You've never seen one?'

'Like the Highwayman's ghost?' He waggled his fingers in front of me and went, 'Whoooo!' He shook his head. 'No, I haven't.'

'Percy, Daniel, get on,' said Mr Magnus.

'Does it have to be night-time to see them? I mean, can you see ghosts in daylight?' I whispered, head down so that Mr Magnus wouldn't see.

'Nah, course not.'

'How do you know if you've never seen one anyway?'

'Hey! You two, on with your work!'

The gowk, wrapped in black cycling gear, was smiling and wheeling a bicycle out of the garage when I got back. 'The Tour de France is coming to the Dales for the Grand Départ. I don't suppose you know what the Grand Départ means, Percival.'

'The big departure?'

I hadn't meant to answer but the words slipped out. Mum had taught me a bit of French. She'd been a teacher in the past.

He looked pleased. 'Good guess. Well done. It's in all the papers. I reckon it's time I got into training; I could ride an *étape* with them. Will you just look at this machine? You'd think it was new, wouldn't you?' he said proudly. 'I take good care of it, always, before putting it away. It's very light, you know. You can lift it with just one finger. Don't you believe me? Try,' he said. 'Go on, try. It won't bite.'

As if I thought a bike would bite! I managed it just, with my middle finger. If I had a bike like that, I could cycle around; I could cycle to Wrath and no one need know.

'Hold it,' he told me. 'I've forgotten my gloves. I'll be back in a moment.'

The minute he was gone inside, I was up on the pedals, whizzing down the path, trying it out.

'Hey! Who said you could ride it? Off!' He was shouting, his eyes all screwed up.

'OK, OK.' I got off, nearly toppling over with the bicycle in my hurry. 'I wasn't doing it any harm.'

'This machine is precious; I asked you to hold it, not ride it.' He looked up at the sky and took deep breaths. When he'd finished, he spoke in a more normal voice. 'Now. I'll be gone for an hour or so. Percival, what will you do while I'm away? Your homework, I hope. What have you got?'

'Countries.'

'Countries!' he snorted. 'What sort of answer is that?'

He didn't wait for me to say anything more, he was back in his good mood. 'Off you go then to your room and do your homework. I might check it when I get back.'

Mum put her head round the bedroom door. 'I'm going to the churchyard. Would you like to come?'

The churchyard where there was grass as green as back at home. The churchyard with the graves that I saw from my bedroom window, the one in my dream. I pulled out my earphones and slid off the bed. 'Why are you going there?'

Below us, we heard the front door open and close.

'Where are you off to?' He was back. He watched us come downstairs.

'To the graveyard. I did tell you.'

'So you did. Must you? That's a pest. I had a puncture, and the kit wasn't where it should be. Someone must have moved it.' He glanced at me. I hadn't. I'd never even seen it. 'Hence my being home early. What a shame you're going out. I was looking forward to at least having the pleasure of your company.'

I held my breath as we crossed the pale wooden floor and reached the front door in case Mum changed her mind. She was putting on her shoes and so I did too, and opened the door.

'I thought you'd like to help me mend my puncture.' He meant me.

I glanced at Mum, hoping she wouldn't say, what a good idea.

'Have you done your homework?' He followed us outside.

'Yes.'

'All of it?'

'Yes.'

'Let's have a look.'

I shook my head.

'Why not?'

'Don't want you to.' I knew he was only trying to keep us there.

'Don't be so mutinous!'

'Oh, do stop it, you two,' Mum broke in. 'Ian, we'll be back soon.'

'Hmm. When?'

'In an hour, I should think,' said Mum.

He looked at his watch, turned his bicycle upside down and started on the tyre. 'At the latest, eh?'

Mum looked irritated, and she didn't speak till we were out of the gate and had crossed the road. 'I met someone yesterday by the beck and we got talking. He looks after one of the flowerbeds in the graveyard and I said I'd help. It's something to do while I'm looking for a job here; I can't keep just making cakes.' She grinned at me.

When we arrived at the lych-gate, a grey-haired man got to his feet to greet us, steadying himself on a tree. 'All right?' he asked Mum.

'Not bad,' Mum answered. 'Yourself?'

'It's a beautiful day,' he grunted. 'Have you come to help, too?' he asked me.

Was I? I wasn't sure.

'Ah. Well, if weeding's not your thing, have a go at the ivy. Get it off the churchyard walls. Pull out the roots if you can.

Rip it out, there's a good lad.'

I went to where he pointed, where ivy crawled up the wall, covering it like a curtain. I tugged. A long skein came off the stones where it had been clinging. Easy. I bent and tried yanking out the roots. That wasn't as easy, until I had the idea that I was pulling out teeth. The gowk's teeth!

'What're you doing here?' Sturdy Harry, from the next table at school, Daniel's friend, was suddenly at my side and pulling too.

'Oh, hiya. She's my mum. Why're you here?'

'That's Granddad. Sometimes I c-c-come and help,' he stuttered. He'd not bothered speaking to me before. 'She's p-pretty, your mum.'

I glanced at her. She was wearing an old flowered frock; her ponytail was coming loose as she worked, and the low sun was catching glints of gold in her hair.

He didn't bother talking to me after that and we tugged in silence. One or two cars passed in the road. The only other sound was voices when people walked past, and birdsong.

'Leave that. C-come with me,' Harry said, suddenly looking mysterious.

I dropped a half-pulled-off streamer of ivy and followed him through a wobbly gate.

'There.'

A stone coffin lay on the ground against the wall of the church tower. It was different from the graves around because it had no lid and it was empty, but someone must have lain in it once, because it was carved out inside in the shape of a head at one end and the shape of a body in the rest.

'Granddad says it's at least six hundred years old.'

'Six hundred! Why isn't there a skeleton in it then?' I challenged.

'I expect it turned to p-powder when they lifted the coffin lid and it b-blew away in the wind.' He thought for a moment. 'Or maybe someone stole it. Lie in it. G-go on. D-dare you.'

'In that?'

'Yes, d-dumbo. Lie in the coffin.'

'What, with my head in the round bit?'

'Yes.'

'Like, now?'

'Yes. G-go on. You're not scared, are you?'

'Course not,' I said quickly.

'Go on then. G-get in.'

I shut my eyes. Maybe the coffin would vanish before I opened them again.

It didn't.

I took a deep breath and stepped in at the foot end.

'Lie down.'

'Do I have to?'

Harry shrugged. 'D-depends.'

'On what?'

'How scared you are.'

'I'm not scared. I told you.' Even so. Lie in a stone coffin where a body had rotted and worms had crawled till it was a skeleton and a skull with grinning teeth?

'Well then.'

Well then, well then. It was only carved-out stone. Empty. Don't think about corpses, don't think about how old it is, don't imagine ghosts. It's stone. That's all. Just stone. But my heart hammered against my ribs.

Harry stood waiting. 'And when you're in it, lying d-down,' he added, 'you have to count t-to ten, out loud.'

Count to ten, I thought. I closed my eyes, took another deep breath, and lay down. My head fitted the head hole and my body was the right length for the body hollow. It was a snug fit. Too snug. My mouth went dry and I had to swallow hard before my voice would come out. 'One,' I croaked. 'Two - three - four - five.' Stone around me, holding me. Its cold crawled into my shoulders and my back. The cold crept on into my arms, my legs, and on into my chest, my tummy. The ice of death. I shuddered. 'Six, seven, eight,' I shouted more loudly, 'nine, ten!'

I jumped to my feet and sprang out. I laughed, it was great to feel grass under my feet. 'I did it! I did it! It wasn't scary,' I lied. 'Have you done it?'

'Me? No way. You're d-daft, you are, lying in there.' But Harry was impressed, I knew he was. 'Absolute d-dumbo!'

I grinned at him. 'Hisshead!' I retorted.

'Scumbag!'

'Prat!'

'P-Pancake!'

'Oy, you two!'

'Yes, Granddad?' Harry called back.

'Where are you?'

'Here.' Harry went to the corner of the church and waved.

'Back to the ivy. No slacking!'

I was about to follow Harry when a tall, wide gravestone caught my eye. It stood on its own, and there was red-and-white plastic tape wound about it. Then I noticed that the tape was wrapped round some of the headstones further along too.

'Are they going to paint the ones with the tape?'

'Paint gravestones? Dunno. I've never seen any painted.'

I liked the idea. The wide one here could be blue, and its writing yellow.

> *To the Memory of the following Children of*
> *William Spencer and Frances his Wife*

A list of names and dates followed:

> *Richard Spencer died 16 Feb 1837 aged 6 months*
> *Anthony Spencer died 24th May 1838 aged 5 weeks*
> *Henry Spencer died 19th May 1841 aged 9 years*
> *William Spencer died 25th Sep 1841 aged 4 weeks*
> *Albert Spencer died 16th March 1848 aged 19 weeks*
> *Mary Ann Spencer died 26th Dec 1854 aged 15 years*
> *William Henry Spencer died 7th Nov 1875 aged 25*

Richard, Anthony, Henry, William, Albert, Mary Ann, I chanted to myself. Children. Turned to dust.

'P-P?' Harry sounded impatient.

'Sshh.' I held up my hand. 'Listen.'

'What?'

I bent back to the stone where it was discoloured and read,

> *He gave thee and took thee, and he will restore thee*

'Can't you hear?'

'Hear what?'

'Oh, nothing.' I shrugged.

But I'd heard laughter. Or was it weeping?

Five

'You heard Mother.' The gowk had come to wake me up again. 'Good morning.'

I turned round in bed. Woody slipped out on to the floor. 'She's not your mother.'

He looked as if he was going to bend down and pick up Woody. I stiffened. But he straightened. He breathed in deeply before he spoke again. 'Up. Breakfast's on the table.'

When I came down dressed, there was none of the parkin that Mum usually put out at the weekend. 'We're cutting back,' he announced, 'as from today. I have to work harder at getting fit. We all do,' he added. 'It's not that your cakes aren't delicious, my precious; they are. But we've been having too many. Muesli and boiled eggs. Plenty.'

Too many cakes? 'I'm not fat,' I complained. Nor was Mum. She looked skinnier than ever. He wasn't fat either. His black shorts and long-sleeved cycling top clung to him like the skin on a snake. There was a small bulge round his middle but that was all.

'Eat, eat,' he ordered, ignoring me and sloshing yoghurt on to three bowls of muesli. 'I'm off cycling. Your mother is driving me to the nearest drop-off point then tracking me.'

'Come with us,' Mum said.

'Yes, you might learn something,' he added. But he didn't really want me with them. I could tell. Besides, there was something in the house I wanted to do.

'I might go round to Daniel's,' I fibbed, with my fingers crossed behind my back.

'Was that the lad in the graveyard?' Mum asked.

'No, his friend,' I said. 'But Harry might be there, too.' It's funny how once you start fibbing, the fibs grow. 'But Daniel's going out first. For about an hour,' I added.

'Perhaps we could trust him with the front-door key in that case, Ian.'

I waited, hoping.

He tapped his foot.

'Ian.'

'Very well then.' He went to the hall drawer. 'Here.' He held up the spare key. 'Don't lose it.'

I tried to take it from him, but he wouldn't let go till I tugged it off him. I put it in my pocket.

'Are you sure it's safe in there?'

I nodded.

'You'll be careful not to break anything while we're away, won't you. Better still, you might like to go to the youth club in town.'

'I'll be at Daniel's,' I repeated. He must have believed me or he'd have thought to ask where Daniel lived.

'Or you could go for a walk.'

'Ian,' Mum said, 'it might come on to rain. Look at that sky.'

'The boy's got rain togs, hasn't he?'

I had. I gulped down some muesli.

'Be careful indoors, no mess. And do be back on time,' he said, 'not like yesterday.'

Mum started to laugh. 'Oh, Ian, we were only about ten minutes late.'

But he wasn't even smiling. Mum looked surprised. 'An hour is an hour; that was what we'd agreed. Never mind.'

'Of course he'll be good,' she said to him. 'Won't you, numkin?' She kissed the top of my head.

As soon as I was sure they were gone, I went to the drawer by the front door. Inside were three keys, lined up side by side. I took them upstairs to the forbidden outside door, drew back the bolts and tried the keys. The first didn't fit. The second fitted but wouldn't turn. The third didn't fit. Under the kitchen sink I found bicycle oil so I took that up and stuck the nozzle in the keyhole and pressed oil out and tried the second key again. It began to turn. More oil, key in, and I turned it. The door shuddered open. I went out on to the top step and glanced around to make sure no one was looking in case they told the gowk, and went down two steps. They were fine. A bit uneven, a bit worn, but not lethal at all. I went back up and shut the door but didn't lock it. I oiled the bolts, top and bottom. Sorted.

I ran downstairs to put back the oil. But I skidded on the polished floor and the can went flying, right bang crack into a china jug displayed on its own on a glass shelf. The jug toppled, fell, and smashed.

My mouth went dry.

I fetched a plastic bag from the drawer and scrambled about picking up the pieces and scrunched up the bag and buried it as well I could under other rubbish in the bin under the sink. I put the keys back in the drawer, laying them side by side as I'd found them, grabbed my jacket and went outside, heart thudding. There'd be trouble.

Six

I slumped on the doorstep. No one passed the gate.

I didn't want to go to any youth club. I wouldn't know anyone there. I couldn't turn up at Daniel's; I didn't know where he lived. Or Harry.

So what then? I got up. I set off along the beck and round the back of the graveyard, heading up away from town, making tracks through the autumn leaves that patterned the pavement gold and red and brown, till I reached a narrow path. It wound up into thick bracken which came right up to my shoulders and stretched beyond and around me like a jungle. I beat my way through it, pretending to be an explorer. Above me the sky was darkening and blobs of rain bombarded my head. By the time I emerged from my jungle you couldn't see where the moors stopped and the clouds began; they were all one. I zipped up my jacket and stopped. I turned in a circle but the cloud was thickening and I couldn't see further than a few steps.

Where was I? Somewhere above Seggleswick, dumbo, I muttered. But where exactly? I'd known the fields and moors round Wrath like the back of my hand; even in cloud I'd have found my way.

Rain trickled down my neck; I wished I had a hood but I'd taken it off and lost it somewhere. I should turn back. But how? I couldn't see the ferns, just tussocks of grass, a rabbit hole and a rocky outcrop. The path had vanished. I didn't fancy scrambling down the steep hill without any path.

A military jet howled overhead behind the clouds. I ducked and slammed my hands to my ears to block out its scream. Two seconds, three, and it was gone. I straightened and walked on up slowly, cautiously. Look for a cairn. Mum had taught me that. A wire fence came up out of the mist.

DANGER!
DEEP EXCAVATIONS
KEEP OUT

I halted, and turned along the fence, keeping it on my left, hoping to see a pyramid of stones that would show I was on the right track. There was none. A tree loomed out of the mist, twisted and withered from past winds, its straggly branches pointy and gnarled like old men's fingers. I was lost. I was wet. I was chilled and I wanted shelter.

I went on. Something solid loomed over to my right, a rock face with an overhang and a shelf below; I could stop there and wait for the mist to clear. As I headed for it, brambles caught my sleeve and held me back. There were blackberries, glistening in the wet and I reached out to pick them. I shovelled them straight in my mouth, squashing them with my tongue, swallowing the tangy juice, then chewing what was left.

Mum liked blackberries. I picked more for her, and put them in a plastic bag from my pocket until it was full. Holding it out above my head with one hand, away from the thorns, I prised off the brambles with the other till I was free of their clutches, then clambered up the rock, sliding and skidding where the rain had made the limestone surface slippery, to the shelf above. It was dry there, sheltered by the rock which curved over my head like a wave about to break.

A wren no longer than my index finger hopped up beside me with a large moth flapping in its beak. The bird swung its head and bashed the insect against the rock wall, and again; it made a crunchy sound. The wren dropped it and placed a claw delicately on it to test that it was dead. Then it started feeding, pausing only to cock its head and watch me watching it. Eat or be eaten, Mum had said once. Did that mean I was like the moth? Nah! Don't be daft.

I tore my eyes away and peered into the mist, but it was denser and I couldn't see a thing. There was only me and the wren, eating. How long would it take for it to stop eating? Or for the mist to clear? I wasn't scared. Not really. I started humming, tapping out a tune on the rock with my fingers and the wren, startled, flew away. I sang more loudly. I remembered tracing those letters in the stone wall B-E-N-J-. I pressed my finger down on the damp rock, B-E- as I sang. I shut my eyes.

I wished I hadn't. I was spinning through space and my stomach lurched. I tried to open my eyes but I was whirling too fast and couldn't. There was a bump, the spinning stopped and I could see.

Voices halloed: 'Benjamin! Benjamin! Where are you?'

'Here!' I shouted back. I was halfway up a rocky slope and

climbing higher, scrabbling on loose stones. An opening gaped in the slope above my head. 'Here!' I shouted again. 'There's a cave!' I squatted on my haunches at its mouth and waited. Four lads joined me; they were my friends.

One stopped close beside me. Unlike us he had no shoes and his shirt was torn and dirty. And he smelt, really bad. 'I'll not go in there,' he said.

'So? Nobody asked you to come with us,' said one of the others.

'We didn't ought to.'

'Go home, Morphet,' said another.

But he stood his ground. 'There's hobs in there.'

'Never!' I retorted. 'Besides, we're on an expedition. Explorers aren't scared of hobs.'

He stared at me, his eyes dark and troubled.

'Hobs don't come out when there are more than three of you. Everyone knows that.' I wasn't absolutely sure that the ancient spirits would leave us alone, but I hoped so. 'There's strength in numbers,' I said stoutly before stooping and going on in before I lost my nerve. I didn't know if he would stick with us or not. He must've followed us up the moor.

Inside, the floor sloped away from us and when I took a step, pebbles rattled down. I followed where they led. 'Candles,' I whispered, swallowing hard, my mouth was so dry. Once our candles were lit, we could see that a narrow passage led off the main chamber. It was low, too, and we had to drop to all fours.

'How do you know where it goes?' came a whisper from behind.

'I don't. Explorers don't know before they try, that's why they're explorers.' I started crawling down the passage. Sharp stones dug into my hands and ripped my woollen trousers. The passage got narrower till it almost squeezed us, and still we crawled. None of us spoke now, not even in a whisper. It was as if we were in the bowels of the earth, miles inside it - and still we went on. We had no choice, we couldn't turn round, the passage was so tight.

It curved sharply to the left.

'Why've you stopped?' someone whispered behind.

I could stand. One by one, the others crawled out and stood up too; we huddled together and held up our candles. In their flickers fantastic shapes sprang out at us.

'See? Hobs!' Morphet hissed, shrinking back.

I reached out and touched one stone shape in the cave wall. 'Not hobs,' I said, 'it's rock. Feel.'

We moved forward cautiously. The light from our candles danced in a pool at the bottom of the cavern. As we skirted round it, I stumbled over something on the cave floor. I crouched down. 'It's a bone!' I scraped at it.

They gathered round. 'It's enormous. That's never human.'

'Look at the curve on it,' one said, 'just like a weapon.'

'It's a tusk!' I remembered a picture seen in a book. 'An elephant's tusk!'

'What, here in Yorkshire?'

'It must be.' I began scraping more earth away from it.

A blob of soil shot up and hit me in the eye.

I blinked it away. It must have hit Morphet too because he grabbed me so as not to fall, and I lurched sideways.

My hair stood on end. I wasn't in any cave, just the same rock shelf. The cloud had lifted and the rain had stopped. And in my hand was not a bone but the edge of a moth's wing. I opened my hand and let it drop.

What was the cave? What had happened? I hadn't been alone either; there'd been friends with me. I kept my head very still and rolled my eyes from side to side to see if anyone else was there. But in the rising mist there was only silence.

Seven

I must have been dreaming, yet it had felt real. I could still smell candlewax and damp earth. That spooked me. I jumped down and tore through the brambles and ran, head down, until wet bracken whipped my face. At least that meant that I was on the right track. I beat my way through the ferns, batting them back, trampling them underfoot, and kept running until at last I reached the beck where I flopped down at the stream's edge. Ducks were waddling through weed in the beck and sliding into the gently flowing water. Watching them swim about in their own small world, my breath slowed and my heart stopped thundering.

'Hey, P.'

'Hiya.' It was Daniel! But by the time I'd registered that, he'd gone on past, whistling. If I'd been quicker, I could've asked to go with him. I could have told him about my dream.

Perhaps Mum was back. I went to the house to see, but she wasn't. I couldn't ring her because she'd never given me a phone. I'd not needed one, she'd said, back then in Wrath. But now we were here, maybe I'd get one for my birthday. I didn't want to go indoors, because of the jug. Anyway, it had stopped raining. I was too warm now in my jacket and I dumped it. I found a ball I'd hidden by the drain and threw it hard against the side wall of the house: ten times straight and catch, ten times throw then bounce, bounce then throw, through my leg, through the other leg, turning between throws, and then with one hand, over and over again, until behind me a car drew up and car doors slammed.

'Hello, love. I'll be with you in a moment,' Mum called out, as she headed for the front door.

I threw the ball once more. It missed the wall and bounced on the window.

The gowk strode up. 'Watch out, you could have broken that! Windows don't come cheap, you know.'

'Sorry,' I said. 'It slipped. It never hit the window before; I 'spect I wasn't concentrating.'

'Indeed. But in any case I'd rather you didn't do that. It makes a racket inside.'

'But you're not inside.'

'We're about to be, aren't we. Besides, it leaves dirty marks. You should have respect for property.' He pointed up at the rough grey stone of the wall.

'I can't see any marks.' I really couldn't.

'Really, Percival! I've had a great day's cycling. Don't spoil it by being cheeky.'

I wasn't being cheeky! If only Mum would come outside again; she'd stick up for me.

'Give us the ball.'

I was so startled, I handed it over.

'Key.'

I handed that over too. He raised his eyebrows. You'd think he was surprised I hadn't lost it. He went indoors, swinging the key, with my ball in his pocket.

I stood there like a banana, not sure what to do. Then I picked up the bag of blackberries for Mum. Inside the door I took off my shoes and set them down.

Oh-oh. He was staring at the empty shelf. He wheeled round when he heard me coming. 'Where's my grandmother's jug?'

'It was an accident.' I should have told him before he saw it. I'd meant to.

'An accident? What do you mean exactly?'

'It fell off and broke.'

'Just like that? You didn't help it?'

I bit my lip. 'Sorry.'

'Sorry isn't good enough. What have you done with the pieces?'

'They're in the bin.'

'In the bin.' He stared at me, tight-lipped. 'An accident. How could you! We leave you in the house and this is what happens.'

'I didn't mean to.'

'Of course he didn't, Ian,' said Mum.

'Your mother and I thought you could be trusted with being left in the house. We thought you would behave your age. I come back to find you trying to break a window, and making marks on the outside of the house…'

I gaped at him.

'…You smash a jug that's precious to me.' There was no stopping him now. 'We didn't expect you to go…'

I turned away. 'Shut your eyes and hold out your hands,' I said to Mum, over his rising voice.

I put the bag in her outstretched hands. The top wasn't

secure and half the berries pushed through and flopped out on the floor.

He snorted. 'Pick them up!'

I knelt and scooped up the berries in my hand. I'd have done that anyway.

'You know where the bin is.'

But Mum was holding out a bowl. 'Here you are. Don't worry. They'll be all right. I'll make us blackberry and apple crumble for pudding, shall I?'

'When those have been on the floor? I don't think so.' He was interfering again.

'The floor's perfectly clean. I washed it after breakfast.'

'I'm not sure he deserves pudding. Throw them away,' he told me. You'd think he hadn't heard her. My heart began pounding with anger.

'Mu-um,' I cried, but she was looking away from me, at him. Inside me something snapped. 'You spoil everything!' I shouted at him, and I burst out crying. I couldn't help it.

I didn't want him to see me cry. I hurled the bowl with its blackberries to the floor. China smashed and skittered over the pale wood. I charged at him, ducked under his arm and was away out of the door before Mum could call me back. I ran down the beck, over the stone-slab bridge, crossed the road, and was round to the back of the church, into the graveyard. I ran until I came to the gravestone which was as tall as me and far wider, the one with all the names I'd seen that time with Harry.

If they came looking, they'd never see me behind it. I'd rushed out, only socks on my feet, there hadn't been time to put on shoes, I'd had to get out of there. I'd gone all cold with fury, it was weird. My teeth were chattering so hard it was like drumming in my brain.

'I hate you!' I shouted. I beat the tombstone with my fists. 'I-hate-you. Ow!' Blood trickled down my knuckles where the skin broke, mingling with the purple blackberry stain. I slumped forward, resting my forehead on the stone. 'I hate you,' I mumbled. My tongue was warm on my hands when I licked the blood. It tasted of metal, mixed with salt from my tears. I turned my back on the tombstone and slid down against it, put my arms round my knees and rocked from side to side on the damp grass of the grave. How could I ever have imagined he could be a father to me? My father wouldn't have been like him. My father wouldn't have fussed about tidiness and not playing ball and eating food off the floor. He'd be cross if I broke a jug but he'd know I'd not meant to. He'd be fair, he'd encourage me, and welcome me, I just knew he would.

How could I go back? They'd be so cross. I rubbed my fists in my eyes and hiccoughed, trying to stop the tears. I leaned my cheek against the cold headstone. Now in the twilight I saw a patch beside me, grave-sized, where the grass grew differently and sunken. Maybe someone was buried under there too and there'd been no one to pay for a headstone. Or no one who wanted to. If I died out here, would they pay for one for me?

They weren't bothering to come looking. No one called my name. If I died out here, they'd be sorry! I ran my finger along the grooves of the writing on the headstone. Richard, Anthony, Henry, William.... They were lucky to have one another. I wished I had a brother; we could hang out together. Not a brother or sister from *him* though, no way. I wished for a friend too. Daniel was OK. So was Harry. Maybe they'd become friends soon.

I heard voices. 'Such peace, the whole place to ourselves. Paradise.'

'Well it would be, if it wasn't spoilt by one thing. Look at those tapes. They're going to flatten the gravestones.'

'Whatever makes you say that?' It was the first voice again, a woman's.

I wiped my eyes on my sleeve and sniffed. I peered round my gravestone.

'Because, my lovely,' answered the man's voice, 'it says so in the lych-gate. Health and safety issues. I expect they think children playing among the graves could be squashed by a toppling headstone.'

I wasn't playing among them!

'Or sheep.' I could see the woman now. She was in a bright green coat that swung open as she walked, and brown hair that curled round her face as she looked up at the other speaker. 'Honestly! I bet no one's ever been knocked over by a headstone in the hundreds of years they've been standing. Why do they think they're dangerous now?'

'Robert John Chevalier, died in 1830. Rest in peace,' the man read out from one of the gravestones.

'How can he rest in peace with that plastic tape round his headstone? It looks as though it's been there for ages, it's so faded. Perhaps you're wrong and it's police tape. Someone's been murdered here, and a corpse is the culprit.'

He barked with laughter. He reached out and hooked a finger into the tape, and pulled it off. 'Well, they'll never find out now. Whatever the reason, Mr Chevalier doesn't want tatty strips of plastic around him, now does he,' he said, balling the tape into his trouser pocket.

'Too right: it's litter!' She giggled. She turned on her heel, glancing round at the cottage windows that overlooked the churchyard to see if anyone was watching. *'Arthur Grundy, died in 1937,'* she read aloud from the next grave. 'He missed the war then.' She reached out, hooked and tore the tape.

They were coming closer. My headstone was one that was taped. If they found me, they'd think I was spying on them, or hiding because I'd done something wrong. They'd see I'd been crying. Quickly, I ripped the tape off my gravestone.

She looked towards the gravestone but I think I ducked in time. They went back to where there were more taped stones, ripping them off as they went and chatting. At last, arm in arm, they left.

Now that the tape was gone, I saw that it had covered another name: *Agnes Spencer died 20th Sept 1847 aged 4 years.*

I read all the names again, trying to work out who'd been born first. It was Henry, born in 1832 when his parents were nineteen. He'd lived till he was only nine and he'd died the same year as his baby brother William. Agnes, died 1847, aged four years. Then Mary Ann Spencer.

He gave thee and took thee, and He will restore thee
And death has no sting

Those words were written in the stone below the list of names. I'd been stung by a bee once. It hadn't been too bad. So dying was even less painful than that?

Mary Ann had at least lived longer, till she was fifteen. I

touched her name on the headstone. My finger tingled, like having pins and needles. It went numb. The headstone and the church tower and the other graves started moving around me, faster and faster like when you're on a roundabout, and then you're spinning and you have to hold on tight so as not to fall. I clutched the headstone, just in time.

'Are you stopping here till the dark falls?' asked a girl standing on the grass beside the headstone. My whirling had stopped. She was wearing a funny-looking smock dress with a pinafore over it.

'Who are you?'

'Why, Mary Ann, of course, Benjamin blue-eyes. Who did you think I was?'

I opened my mouth, about to say, I'm not Benjamin, but shut it again quickly. It was only the second time I'd been called that, ever, but it was one of my names, and I did have blue eyes.

'Come, you promised.' She held a hand out to me and, dazed, I took it. 'You'd not want to fall in.'

Fall in? I turned to look. Right beside me was a deep hole and the headstone was flat on the ground alongside a heap of fresh earth. The hole was deep and there was straw laid down at the bottom.

'Benjamin, are you sickening?' She peered at me. 'Please come! You have to. I've no brothers left on earth and now my only sister has gone to heaven, too. She coughed her heart and soul out, Mother said, with the chincough. So you can pretend you're my brother, can you not?' She was tugging my hand. Clack, clack went the wooden soles of her clogs on the gravestone path; my damp socks made no sound at all.

In the church porch, stone benches ran along the two walls. She went to the end of one, knelt with her ear to the great oak door, and beckoned me over. As I put my cold cheek next to her hot one to listen, I could see tears well up in her eyes.

On the other side of the closed door came the deep voices of men singing. When they finished, someone spoke. It sounded like praying.

Then there was silence. Mary Ann got to her feet and lifted the heavy iron latch. 'Help me, I want to see.' I got off the bench and we eased back the door, just an inch. A priest came walking slowly down the aisle towards us. Behind him was a man with a large box on his shoulder, draped in black cloth: a child-sized coffin. His face was closed tight, as if he was trying not to weep. A small procession of men in black overcoats carrying black hats came on behind.

I swung the door wide open for them as they drew near. The priest passed through and then the man with the coffin. He stopped, and the men behind stopped too. 'Go home, Mary Ann,' he said. 'I told you not to come. Funerals are no place for a girl.'

'But Benjamin is with me, Father.'

Her father's eyes swept right over me. He looked puzzled. 'Well, if you left the lad outside, fetch him and let him take you home. Your mother will need help in preparing the funeral tea.' He followed the priest.

The other men passed through, not singing now, not talking. Their heels clicked on the stone graves of the porch floor, their clothing whispered as they reached up to put on their tall black hats, and out they went.

'He didn't see me,' I said.

'He had other things on his mind,' Mary Ann said. She was framed in the porch, looking back at me. 'Come on.' I took a step but my foot seemed to land on a snail because I heard a small crack under my foot and felt something squelch and a jolt go through my foot. She was turning, her outline black against the darkening sky and then what I was seeing somersaulted and whirled and my world turned black.

Eight

Next thing I knew, someone was shaking my shoulder.

'What's a lad like you doing, huddled up here in the church porch, haven't you a home to go to?' He was wearing a long cloak. It must be the priest. But he wasn't the same priest as - when? where? My teeth chattered.

'Where have you come from?' he asked.

I glanced at the oak door. It was open but there was no sign of men in black overcoats and black hats, no sign of any father with a coffin on his shoulder. Nor in the opening of the porch was there any girl in a smock and pinafore. I looked warily at him.

'I'm Alan. I'm the vicar here,' he said. 'What's your name? I haven't seen you before, have I? Where have you sprung from?'

'Wrath,' I answered at last.

'What, today? That's miles! Did you walk all the way?'

'Yes. I mean, no. I walked from the beck.'

'Not far then. Ah, I remember now.' He clicked his fingers. 'Ian Bockley's place, I assume. I heard that you and your mother have joined him, eh? A small family. We used to see Ian out and about a lot on Sundays on his bicycle; not so much recently,' he mused, 'I expect that's why. It's well past supper time. Shouldn't you be going home?' He made shooing signs at me, as if I was a chicken.

I tugged off my socks and, clutching them in a wet ball, I fled.

'Where were you?' Mum came running out of the house as I kicked the gate closed behind me. 'I came out and called but you didn't answer. I looked everywhere for you. I know Ian was angry, but he was fond of that jug.'

'I didn't mean-'

'Hush. I know you didn't. But you shouldn't have gone off like that, I've been so worried.'

'He took my ball too, Mum.'

'Come on, love. You're shivering. Let's get you to bed.'

She put her arm round me and led me upstairs as if I was little again. I didn't mind. It was good to feel that Mum cared after all. The gowk didn't appear. I was confused and tired, so tired.

In my room she took my dirty, wet socks off me then sat back on her heels. 'I do so wish that you would try to get on with Uncle Ian.' She looked sad.

'He hates me.'

'No, he doesn't.'

'He does.' I climbed into bed and turned away from her.

She sighed. 'I'll come and pick you up after school, shall I?'

Please yourself, I thought.

She looked down at me. 'If you've caught a chill, you'd better stay in bed for a couple of days.'

'No!' I didn't want to stay in this house if I didn't have to. 'Mum?' I humped round to face her.

'Yes, love.'

'Let's go home.'

The bed dipped as she sat on it. She put a hand on mine. 'Don't be silly. I gave up the cottage, you know that.'

'We can find another.'

'In Wrath? There isn't another to rent.'

'We'd find one. You could get your old job back at the farm shop, and we could stay with Kath on the farm. It'd be great.'

'Kath has her own family to think of.' Mum wasn't smiling.

'And I could have a bike. It could be second-hand, I wouldn't mind, honest. Please, Mum. Let's go home.'

She tucked the sheet around me, frowning. 'Percy, listen. School's all right, isn't it? You're getting on fine there, aren't you?'

I hesitated before nodding. I wasn't being bullied, and being called P no longer seemed to matter, especially when it was really just P. But that wasn't the point. I didn't belong here; I had no friends. I loved Mum all right but it was her fault that we were stuck here.

'And you like your room here at home, don't you? I got that right for you, didn't I?'

I sat up and threw off her hand. 'It's not home! You're not to call it home!'

'Ssh! Keep your voice down.'

'Why do we have to live with him?' I was still shouting. I didn't care.

'Because it wouldn't have made sense for him to live with us. He owns this house and we were renting. Besides, Wrath has no shops and no station.'

'But why do we have to live with him anyway? We were happy before.'

'Because, numkin, I love Ian, and he loves me.'

'So?'

'That's enough.' Her voice sharpened. 'When you're older, you'll understand. Come on now, settle down.'

But I stayed sitting up. I didn't want to understand.

'Goodnight then.' She kissed me and turned off the light.

I lay wide awake in bed. Through the wooden boards of the floor I could hear them downstairs. I pulled back the curtains. The moon lit up the graveyard so brightly that the headstones and their shadows were as sharp as knives. It was so clear that I could almost see the writing on the gravestones. I stared, in case anything moved down there. I couldn't see the Spencer gravestone from here, or any girl but she'd have gone home anyway.

I fell back on the pillows. Why had I seen her? *'He will restore thee.'* So was she being restored, like it said on the gravestone? Would I see her again?

It'd felt as if I'd belonged. Like before, in the cave. But belonged where?

A cloud drew over the moon, like a blanket being pulled up across my window, and I shut my eyes, and fell right into a dream. I was being smothered by ferns. They were closing over my head, warm and damp and sticky. But I burst through and ran downhill and there was a lad at my side, the smelly one, and a man was chasing us and gaining on us, and shouting, 'Morphet, come back, yer brat.' Just as we were running into the market square, something woke me. Woody was on the windowsill; when I'd fallen asleep he'd been on the chair at my side. My curtains had been drawn again. Mum must've come back; my bedroom door was closing again.

I was wide awake now. Outside, the moonlight was still so bright it was like daytime only without the colour. I got out of bed and stood in front of the forbidden outer door. Slowly I pulled back the top bolt, then the bottom. I opened the door. All was still. The night air was cool on my face.

I fetched Woody. I went down the steps in my pyjamas, all the way to the bottom. Nothing moved. I shivered, but didn't go back. I walked through the garden and on to the lane along the beck. Sharp stones stabbed my feet but I carried on, down the lane to the road. I crossed it and stood at the open gate to the churchyard. Nothing stirred.

Boom!

I turned and ran.

Boom!

Back – boom! – down the lane. Three o'clock. It was only the church clock sounding. An owl shrieked nearby. My heart thudded like a drum and I tore up the steps and back indoors. Next time I would be braver. Next time.

Nine

Church bells ringing woke me up. Sun poured in through the window. Yes! No school today.

Then I remembered where I was. All the same, I got up before I was fetched.

'Hurry, Percival. We're going on a family walk this morning,' the gowk said when I came down. 'Quality time,' he said brightly, putting a boiled egg and toast in front of me, for a change.

'That'll be nice, won't it, pet? You like walking, and it's a beautiful day.'

I did like walking. I liked it best when it was Mum and me. Or with my friends at home. Or roaming about on my own. I bashed the top of my egg and cut it off. 'Do I have to come?' I asked Mum.

'You most certainly do,' he answered. He was being all jolly.

We crossed the river and went into town and started going up the steep street the other side of the market square. 'Before Queen Victoria's diamond jubilee this was called Warehouse Hill,' he told us. 'Imagine, there were plenty of shops here then: butchers, bakers, suchlike.' I dawdled along behind. Further up, the road narrowed between walls and was cobbled. The roundness of the stones fitted nicely into the hollow of my foot. The gowk fell back till he was alongside. 'Something else interesting,' he said, all chatty and friendly, 'about cobbles. I have a colleague who's Dutch, and do you know what they call them in the Netherlands? *Kinderkoppen.*' He lowered his voice. 'I bet you don't know what *kinderkoppen* means.'

Of course I didn't. I shook my head.

'Children's heads! Imagine that!'

He strode back to Mum, chortling, leaving me on the cobbles. 'What's so funny?' I heard her ask.

'Oh, just a bit of folklore I was telling the boy.'

I looked down at my feet and felt sick. It was narrow here. There was no pavement, just the high wall of the house on my left. I sprang to the edge of the road and walked on up sideways like a crab, hugging the wall, I didn't like the idea of treading on other children's heads. But when I clung to the wall for support, it sent out a stench that made my stomach churn. I could smell dead, rotting animals and urine. So I let go and tried to go on crab-walking in order to take up as little space and avoid as many cobbles as possible. It was difficult to walk like that and keep my balance. When the gowk turned and saw what I was doing, he got Mum to turn too. She looked puzzled, but I suppose she thought I was playing some secret game because I saw her smile when he said something to her, and she let him tuck her arm back in his before walking on.

I managed to get through the stretch of cobbles without overbalancing. When I turned to look, the wall was glowing in the sunshine, and I couldn't understand why it had been stinking so. The cobbles, too, they were just cobbles.

I trudged behind them, up a lane and eventually, when that

petered out, on to the moor among the grazing sheep. It was like sitting in the back of the car; in the front he and Mum would be talking but I could be alone in the back with my own thoughts. Now they were holding hands. 'Meh!' bleated a sheep at the side. 'Meh!' Our eyes locked as it chewed, its jaw sliding from side to side. It bent its head and went back to ripping up grass.

It wasn't too bad out there with the moors and crags stretching out around. They were so vast, they made him look tiny and less important. The moors and the hills and the rocks were there before he'd ever been born. They'd still be there when he was dead. By the time we scrambled up to reach Victoria Cave I was almost cheerful.

At the dark entrance he took out a leaflet and read, his voice ringing out over the moor. 'Here they found the bones of mammoth, bear, reindeer, hippopotamus, giant deer, rhinoceros and lion, among others, left behind from thousands of years before.'

He'd left out elephant. I remembered elephant.

'Other, more recent, finds include Bronze Age pottery, Roman jewellery, tools and coins from before 400 AD. Hey!' He yanked me back by my collar. 'Where do you think you're going?'

'Inside.' Wasn't it obvious?

'Oh no, you're not. You'll dirty your clothes. Don't gape at me like that. You can be so selfish. Do you think your mother has got nothing better to do than wash your clothes?'

'Oh, I don't mind.' Her hair was blowing about her face and her cheeks were pink and glowing. 'But you'd need a torch, wouldn't you; it'll be dark in there.'

He jabbed a walking pole into the ground. 'It's not safe. I'm not prepared to accompany you, and nor is your mother. You could have an accident; I don't want to have that on my watch now, do I? So stay with us. We'll go on another half hour and then have our sandwiches. How about walking with us, and making conversation, hmm? No more trailing along behind.'

I let his words wash over me, hearing Mum's mention of a torch. It hadn't been torchlight, it had been candlelight! I'd been in here already. I seemed to hear laughter and the sound of small stones falling, as when someone's climbing down. It had been me. There'd been friends with me, too. I surged forward into the mouth of the cave.

'Percival! Come back here! At once!'

I did turn back. Mum reached out and squeezed my hand. She was looking tired and sort of thoughtful. The gowk went on talking and no one answered, and the sandwiches, when we came to eat them on the moorside, were flabby and tasted of nothing at all.

Ten

'Percival!'

We were back after the walk, and I had Lego spread out over the landing. I came to the top of the stairs and looked down.

'What's this?' Red-and-white tape drooped from the gowk's hands. 'I was putting out the rubbish and look what I found. Well, what is it?'

'Plastic tape?'

'Exactly, plastic tape. What's it doing in our rubbish bin?'

'Dunno.' I'd never thought it'd be noticed in the bin.

'I think you do. I'm sure your mother won't have put it in, and I didn't, so it must have been you.'

'Why? Anyone could have dropped it in there.'

He narrowed his eyes. 'Not many people go past our back door,' he said drily. 'Did you put it in?'

'Me? No.' I crossed my fingers behind my back.

'Come here.'

I went downstairs as slowly as I could. When I reached the bottom step we were so close our noses almost touched.

He took my arm and marched me to the centre of the room. 'Wait.' He fetched a kitchen stool and set it down.

'What've I done wrong?' I stared at him, trying to nail him

with my eyes, my heart beating fast and high. I'd only copied what the couple had done.

'What have you done wrong? Look here, young man: that tape is either police scene-of-crime tape, or else it's health-and-safety tape. Either way, it shouldn't be tampered with. Where did you take it from?' A vein stood out on his forehead. I could see it throbbing. 'Sit! You will stay there until you confess and apologise.'

'Anyone could have put it there,' I repeated, 'it doesn't have to have been me.' I wasn't going to tell him; I didn't want him going into the graveyard. The graveyard was my place, my secret.

I didn't like it, in the middle of the room, just sitting on the stool, not knowing what he'd do. I'd never seen him so angry. I'd pushed him too far. Where was Mum? I hummed quietly so as not to cry. Upstairs I could hear him clearing away the Lego. Again. He came down and went outside.

'Mum?' I called, but there was no answer. I didn't dare move. A cobweb distracted me, dangling from a window catch. He couldn't have noticed it or he'd have wiped it away in a flash. It swayed gently in a draught, held in place only by two strands of silken thread. A tiny fly struggled in the corner of the web, trying to break free of the sticky stuff. The spider was an inch away from it, waiting. I couldn't tear my eyes away.

I was still seated there when Mum came back.

'Hello, love. What are you doing there?'

'Sitting.'

'Well, I can see that, pet. But why?'

'He's there until he apologises.'

I jumped. I hadn't heard him come in. He must have spotted

Mum returning. 'Either he apologises for lying, or he admits to putting the tape in the bin.'

'Tape? What tape, Ian?'

'Ask him.'

I bit my lip, hard.

'Stubborn as a mule, that one. Come on, the two of us'll have our tea.'

'Oh, surely Percy can have his tea with us.'

'Percival can have his tea when he's said what he has to say.'

Mum frowned. 'I really think...' she began.

'Don't bother. He'll come round. You'll see.'

Never, I thought. I didn't speak when the smell of cauliflower cheese wafted over. Mum came over to me.

'Leave him be. He has to learn.'

'No, Ian,' she defied him, 'not this way. Come on, love, come and eat.' She took my hand and led me to the table. I didn't speak as I ate. I didn't speak as I left half the cauliflower on my plate.

'Either you stay here till you finish your supper, and I don't care how long that takes – or you go to bed, now,' he said.

Fine. I pushed away the plate, got to my feet, and went straight upstairs.

As I closed the bedroom door, I heard him say, 'No, stay here,' to Mum.

'He's not a bad lad. You're being too hard on him.'

'He's turning into a little criminal; we must nip such tendencies in the bud.'

'Oh, Ian, Percy, a criminal? Isn't that rather an over-reaction? There have been a lot of changes in his life, he's bound to be feeling unsettled. I want to...'

'Leave him be. Trust me. We mustn't make excuses for him. If we let him get away with this, there's no telling what he could do next. The boy has to learn. Besides, he's winding me up. Deliberately, I'm sure of it.'

I shut my door and sat on the bed. I bet Daniel and Mary Ann weren't in their bedrooms now. Or Harry. Or Tim.

I crept back to the door and listened. Silence.

There was a cloth ball on my shelf. I grabbed it and flung it against the wall, caught it, threw it, caught it, threw it, caught-

It landed on the floor between us. The gowk stood in the doorway. Slowly he shut the door and stood in front of it, breathing heavily. He didn't move.

I stared at him defiantly. I didn't blink. I didn't look away.

He bent and picked up the ball. He glared at me and went out with it. 'Shut the door behind me.'

I waited till I heard he was at least halfway down the stairs before I shut it. My legs were trembling. I sat on the bed and waited till they stopped. Then I turned and knelt at the window, my elbows on the sill. I stared at the sheepy bank, thinking. I picked it up and rattled it, but I knew all it had inside was £1.50, and that wasn't enough to run away. What if I ran away to the other life?

I set the china sheep down and looked out, brooding. The sun had gone in and now everything looked grey: the houses and walls, the paths, even the trees, the moors beyond and the cloudy sky. All looked as grey and glum as my heart. At last Mum came in. She closed the door behind her and sat down on the bed.

'He's well out of order, Mum.'

She pulled the scrunchy off her hair and shook it free.

'Mum.'

'Come here.' She put her arm round me. 'I want to think.'

'He hates me.'

'Don't be silly. I've told you before, of course he doesn't hate you.'

'He does! You should hear what he says when you're not there.'

'What does he say?'

'He...' It was complicated; I didn't know how to explain.

She sighed. 'Percy love, what I see is someone not yet used to boys.'

Yet. She'd used the word yet. 'Mum, he really has it in for me,' I said urgently.

'Enough! I sometimes think you have it in for him, too.' Her voice softened. 'I'm trying to sort this out, trying to make it work for us all. We just have to get used to each other, like pieces in a jigsaw waiting to fit together. It may take us a little while. Ian's going to try. Will you try, too? Will you, please, for my sake?'

'What's the point!'

'Percy?'

Eventually I grunted a sort-of yes. For her.

'Thank you.' She tucked me in and kissed me.

When she was gone, I knelt up at the window again. I'd try praying. I folded my hands and screwed my eyes closed. Please God, help, I whispered. Make him ill or something. Let him have an accident and go away to hospital.

I opened my eyes quickly. I didn't think you were meant to pray that way. I didn't add Amen. I watched as clouds began to break up. I watched as the sunset slashed across them, pink and purple. I watched the sky fade into darkness, and then the answer came to me. I had to curse him, not pray. I knew the best place to do it. Mary Ann had said that I was brave. Could I dare?

At last I heard them come upstairs. Under cover of their bathroom sounds I slipped off the bed and unbolted the outside door, top and bottom. I waited again till I heard their bedroom door click shut. Then I pulled a jumper over my pyjamas and eased back the bolts, grabbed Woody and crept down the stone steps. Light shone from one upstairs window as I walked along the beck but I didn't need it to show the way; the moon was bright enough. I crossed the slab bridge over the beck, and then the empty road, and reached the churchyard. I stepped from the shelter of the gate, and on to the grave-slab path. 'Hello,' I whispered, and I paused, in case anyone was there. All was silent, and the gravestones shone in the moonlight. I picked my way past them to get to the open coffin. It was dark, shaded by the tower above from the moon's beams. I couldn't see if there was a body in there. I held my breath. I made myself look. It was empty. Was I meant to lie in it to say a curse? I wouldn't. I couldn't. But I did bend down and touch it. I swallowed hard. 'Make the gowk ill. Ian Bockley is his name. Make him go away,' I whispered. Something fluttered past my ear, brushing my hair, and whirled blackly into the sky, making me gasp. It must have been a bat, with its sonar switched off. I squeezed Woody tightly to me and rushed to the Spencer grave, rested my hand on its headstone for comfort, to make my heart stop jumping. I tore a handful of grass from the grave and ran back to bed, still clutching it.

Eleven

But it wasn't night-time. It was afternoon, and I was running, running because I wanted to get home. A door opened as I ran across the square and reached the corner.

'I'm right glad you're back, our Benjamin.' It was Mother, in her long brown dress, half covered by an apron. 'You can save me a trip. Will you go and find Morphet? I have made a stew for him and his father. Don't wrinkle up your nose,' she said sharply. 'He is not as fortunate as you.'

There are plenty not as fortunate, I muttered as I went off to where Morphet lived. Hah! I'd wanted to help Father in the shop, in with the deep smell of leather and wax, meeting the customers, but no, I had to go and find Morphet when I'd rather play with my friends. I passed the pubs with the men lounging outside, smoking and drinking; I passed the track leading to the town well, passed the Folly with its elaborately carved doorway and barefoot children playing outside, and turned into the yard of the tenement building.

Morphet was on his knees. His father was thrashing him with a stick like I'd not seen before, it was so thick. With each blow, Morphet rocked.

How could he stay kneeling and not fall to the ground?

Tears ran down his cheeks but he didn't cry out.

Thud, thud, went the stick.

I whirled and ran down the street, round the back of our house, into the kitchen. Mother was lifting a dead chicken from her basket. 'You must come!' I gasped. 'He's killing him.'

She didn't ask 'Who?' She dropped the chicken on to the table and followed me, still in her apron. I had to keep stopping for her to catch up. I didn't want to get there on my own, frightened at what I might find.

We entered the dirty courtyard together. Morphet was gone. His father was gone. We stopped. Mother looked around.

We both heard it. Choking sobs. We couldn't see where it came from.

'Pray God, no!' Mother darted over to the dark corner.

There, shut in a pigsty, was Morphet.

Mother rushed over to the door of their house and hammered on it. 'Morphet's father, come out! Come out, Amos Bibber!'

'You can break the door down, missus, and shout out your lungs, but you'll not get him.' Two women had come out and were watching. 'He's gone. It's a disgrace!'

'It is, Ma Cox,' said Mother. 'That's exactly what it is.' She drew back the bolt that fastened the wire door to the pigsty and held out her hand to Morphet. 'Come, let's get you cleaned up,' she said softly.

He shrank back. Tears and snot were smeared across his cheeks.

'I'll not harm you. I dare say you'd like something to eat.'

Inch by inch she coaxed him out of the pigsty. She put her arm round his shoulders.

He doubled up and retched thin stuff, right at her feet.

I lay in bed, rigid, listening. Someone was being sick, and it sounded like Mum. I pulled back the bedclothes and went out on to the landing just as she was coming out of the bathroom.
'Mum?'
'It's all right, pet. Back to bed with you. I must have eaten something. Come on now, it's almost morning, back to sleep.'
She led me to bed and tucked me up. I watched the door.

Twelve

The door wasn't closing at all. It was opening and not into darkness but into daylight, and it wasn't my bedroom door. I was back in scratchy woollen trousers and the wooden soles of my shoes clattered as I darted out of Father's shop to greet a man who halted his horse at our door.

'Fine day,' he observed from his height in the saddle.

'Aye, sir, it is, if you're on a horse. Not if your feet are in the mud.' I grinned at him.

'Impudent young scamp!' He raised his whip. But seeing someone behind me, he lowered it. 'You need to curb your son's tongue, Mr Waugh. Good morning.'

'Good morning, Mr Moore. Young Benjamin here was just telling me about an ancient bone he found in a cave up on the moors. An elephant's tusk, maybe.'

'Elephant's tusk: pshaw!' Farmer Moore dismounted and handed the reins to me. 'There are no elephants up this way, lad. You need to go to Africa for elephants.'

'Or to India,' I told him, tying the reins to the iron ring in the wall. His horse started and tossed his head at me. 'Whoa.' I clicked my tongue at it. 'And it did look like the tusks I've seen in pictures,' I said to the big-bellied man.

'Don't go spinning tales, lad.'

'I'm not. It's true!' I cried.

'Benjamin,' Father warned me. Quietly he said, 'Go inside and find your mother. Grace is spending the afternoon with your aunt; with this baby on the way your mother needs more help than usual.'

'He's a chip off the old block all right!' I heard Mr Moore say as I went into the dark interior. 'Like his father, always arguing.'

'Aye. Yet it is no bad thing for a lad to have a lively mind. He could be right, you know. Folk are talking about ancient finds in caves round here. And there's that book that's been published in Edinburgh which tells of such things…'

'Books, eh. No need for 'em, never read 'em. Full of dangerous ideas. Elephant tusks in Yorkshire, a likely tale!' Mr Moore spluttered.

I didn't hear any more after that but went on through the back of the shop to the parlour. It was dark in there but for an arrow of sunlight that pierced the mullioned window and made specks of dust dance in the air before it hit the blue and white cups that hung from hooks on the black oak dresser. Sounds were coming from the open door to the kitchen. Mother was at the sink, with Morphet. She was rubbing a wet cloth over his face and hands and neck.

'What did you do to make your father so angry?' she was asking him.

'I was up on t' moor.'

'There's no sin in that.' He squirmed as she scrubbed harder. 'Hold still. Another time, you come straight to us. I don't want to find you shut up in the pigsty again.'

'He's smelly enough already!' I teased.

'Benjamin!' She whirled round to me. 'He can't help it. If you collected muck for the tannery you'd soon smell of it, too.' She piled a plate high with bread and cheese and handed it to Morphet. 'Sit quietly and eat that, and I'll tell you a story. You sit too, our Benjamin.'

She went to her chair, put the dead chicken on her aproned lap and began plucking its feathers into a bowl at her feet, softly singing one of her favourite songs, 'I know that my redeemer liveth'. 'Now then, that's by the famous Mr Handel. Shall I tell you about the time I went all the way in the coach to Huddersfield with Benjamin's father to hear Mr Handel's "The Messiah"? Benjamin knows the story already.'

I laughed. I'd heard it so many times, I knew it like the back of my hand. It was from before I was born. The outing hadn't been with my father alone; there'd been others sitting inside the coach and outside. 'That was the night I decided that if the saddler from Seggleswick asked me to marry him, I'd say yes,' she ended, as I knew she would. 'Done. Look.' She held the now-bald chicken up for inspection. 'One of your father's customers brought it when he came to pay for his saddle. John, no!'

My four-year-old brother had hold of some feathers and was trying to stuff them into Jane's mouth, but Mother was there first. 'Collect the feathers, our Benjamin, would you?' she asked. 'And you, Jane,' she said, brushing down my six-year-old sister. 'You should know better than to encourage young John. Morphet, have you finished? Off you go then. Take the stew!' she called after him. He came back and took it from her and scarpered, as if he was scared we'd take it off him.

While I gathered up the feathers and put them in an old pillow case, and shooed away Polly the cat who was batting loose feathers in the air with her paw, Mother went to the sink and reached inside the bird and pulled till its entrails slithered out. She wrapped them in a sheet of old newspaper before washing the chicken and wiping her hands dry on her apron. 'Jane, you come and help me prepare the vegetables and, Benjamin, will you take round the coal for me? I'd come with you, but I'm a bit tired. I'm not so strong at carrying things just now.' She rested her hands on her swollen belly. 'Benjamin, you be kind to that Morphet.'

'I *am*.' And in that moment I was sorry I'd been mean. I would be kind.

She looked sharply at me. 'Good. Because he's got no one.'

'Boy!'

'Go on, your father's calling you. Go and see what he wants. And take that cat with you!'

'Polly, here, Poll.' She miaowed loudly in protest as I picked her up. Back in the shop, Mr Moore was gone.

'Cheeky skat!' Father reached out to cuff me.

I grinned and ducked just in time, dropping Polly. The bell on her collar jangled as she fell. She scampered outside.

'Hmm.' He looked fierce. 'It's good to stand up for yourself, you're right to do so. But we'll have less of your lip with the customers, do you hear? I do not wish to lose Mr Moore's custom because of you. Now, are you going to stay and help?'

'Will it do later? Only Mother's asked me to take round coal. To her poor,' I added.

'They're our poor too, lad, and don't you forget it, and they've got names and all.' His face softened. 'I suppose it can wait an hour. Until the baby comes, she'll need your help just as much as I do. She's not having it easy this time. The wheelbarrow's out the back.'

In the yard I took the shovel and dug it into the heap of coal until the barrow was piled high. Going back to the tenements this time took longer what with the weight of the wheelbarrow and the steep hill. Twice I had to press to the wall to get out of the way of the pack ponies strung together and struggling downhill, bells tinkling, their bags bulging on either side, full of wool and skins from hill farms. Twice I had to pick up lumps of coal where they fell from the wheelbarrow tipping over a bit at the side of the road. There was no sign of Morphet or his father by the time I crossed the muddy, smelly yard. I called into the dark room of the first home and shovelled the coal into the buckets the women there came to give me. The next one was Welly Cox's wife. She only had one bucket. I filled it as full as I could even though she scowled at me. Then there were two more. The barrow was soon empty. Most of the women asked me to thank Mother, and when one even curtsied to me, I blushed.

Mother was waiting back at our kitchen door with the two large water jugs. 'Have you done?'

'They asked me to give you their thanks. Except that Ma Cox. She's a right sourpuss.'

'Do not speak that way of your elders! Mrs Cox has a hard life with a husband like Welly, off all hours drinking with Morphet's father. I wouldn't wonder if....' Her voice trailed away. 'Never mind that. Will you fetch water now?'

I went up the track to two stone water troughs. No one was waiting. I dipped in one jug, close to where the water bubbled up from an underground spring, and when it was full hoisted it out with both hands it was so heavy. 'Benjamin's no good at sparking,' scoffed one of my friends, to the clatter and scrape of clogs behind me. The others laughed. I put down the jug I'd been about to fill.

'I am! I'm the best!' I ran a few steps downhill and swung my foot hard against a cobble. Sparks flew from the iron ridge on the sole of my clog. 'Yeh!' I shouted. 'Now, in a line: one-two-three!' We took a run and scraped all together. It made a fair racket and we cheered as the sparks flew. Morphet couldn't do this if he tried; not with his bare feet. We did it again and again till one lad's mother called him and the rest of us scattered.

Thirteen

Watching the clouds scud across the sky, chased by a flock of crows, black against the blue, I felt weird after the dreams of the last nights. If they had been dreams. I didn't know. I didn't want to go to school. Or stay here. I had a hollow where my stomach should be.

At breakfast we were all quiet. Mum rested her elbows on the table, pressed her thumbs into the side of her eyes, closing them. I watched her carefully as I bolted my food. You'd think she had a headache.

'Off already?' She stirred as I got up from the table, and hugged me goodbye.

Kyle and Harry came into the school grounds together, heads together, talking. They started kicking a ball around.

'Hiya, Harry,' I said.

I don't think he heard me. When Daniel arrived, he ran straight over and joined them. I didn't hang back any longer; I'd break in and practise curving balls with them.

But the whistle blew and I never made it.

'Freeze!' called the teacher on duty.

I stopped on one foot, quickly spreading my arms for balance.

'Right. Line up. Hush. Darren, stop telling tales. You lot, leave that ball where it is.'

I joined my class line, behind a girl with a thick pigtail the colour of straw. I hadn't noticed her before.

She turned her head. 'You're P, aren't you? I've heard about you.'

I blushed and nodded.

'Is P really your name?'

'Not really, it's Percy. But Daniel calls me P. So do the others. I don't mind.' I shrugged.

'Okeydoke. Well, I'm Maryann.' She faced me, her back to the teacher on playground duty. Her face was pale but her brown eyes danced and sparkled. 'I've been away. They had to take out my appendix. I'm OK now. That's why I wasn't in class.'

'Marianne?' I checked her name.

'No, Mary Ann.' She separated the two words. 'Why are you looking at me like that?'

'Your name.'

'What's up with it?'

'Nothing. It's, um, pretty.' I blushed again.

'Harry told me about you. Lying in a coffin.'

'Mary Ann, turn round and follow,' said the teacher.

In class, she pulled out the chair opposite Daniel and me which had been empty, and sat. When she smiled, there was a gap in her front teeth.

'We're going to do root words this morning.' Mr Magnus tapped at his keyboard then pointed at the screen hanging on the wall. 'Open your books, page fifty-three. But first, would anyone like to hazard a guess as to what a root word is? Percy?

Percy Waugh?'

'Wuff! Wuff!'

I glared round the class. 'It's not Wuff, it's War. D'you hear? War!'

They looked startled. I even got a grin from Harry.

'Right-o, Percy *War*. I'll repeat the question,' said Mr Magnus. 'Do you have an idea as to what a root word is?'

I stared at words on the screen but couldn't concentrate because of Mary Ann. Not just because she knew about the coffin. I could still feel the cold of that stone. I could still see it, shadowed in darkness last night. No, it was because I'd met her before - except, I couldn't have. 'Not really,' I said.

Mr Magnus ignored the hands that were waving in the air. 'Mary Ann Spencer?'

Spencer!

'The letters that look the same?' she asked.

'That's it.' He underlined re<u>serve</u>, <u>serv</u>ice, <u>serv</u>er, re<u>serv</u>ed. 'The root word can be in the middle, or at the beginning or at the end, do you see? Just now Percy said "not really". Here on the board, what have we got? Really, reality, unreal - so what would be the root word there? Yes, Harry.'

'Real,' said Harry.

What was real? Harry, winking at me and jabbing at his head with a finger as if to say I was crazy? Had I really shovelled coal and fetched water for someone I called Mother and helped someone I called Father? In that other world I belonged. I had friends there, too. And what about the funeral? Who were Mary Ann and Morphet? And which Mary Ann Spencer, this one or the one in the graveyard? This classroom was real enough, and Mr Magnus, and my classmates. I peered at

Louise, wondering if I could make her disappear. She stuck her finger on her nose and crossed her eyes at me.

The gowk might not be real.

But he was. Then I started on thinking about Mum. Why was she being sick in the night?

'That's it. In your books, you're given a word, the root word. This time I want to you to make longer words from it. We'll do one together. Act.'

'Action?' Daniel called out.

'Good. Any more – someone else? What words can you make with act? Percy? Wake up! Come back to the land of the living!'

'Reaction? And react?' Maybe there was some way I could react to the gowk so that he went, disappeared, *paf*! In a dream you can sometimes make things happen. It could work.

'I was thinking those,' Louise called out.

'You may have *thought* them, but Percy *said* them. So: write down as many words as you can think of from the root words in your book. Discuss, talk, debate. Josh, you're already writing? Oh, don't wait for us then, just keep going. The rest of you, off you go.'

I did get on with the exercise; that at least was real.

At lunch I was finishing my jacket potato with tuna when Mary Ann came and sat beside me. 'You're right brave,' she said.

'Am I?'

'Lying in a coffin. It could be cursed.'

I put down the spoonful of sticky-toffee pudding that was halfway to my mouth and stared at her. 'Why d'you say that?'

She shrugged. 'That's what everyone says. Weren't you scared?'

I shook my head and went on eating to hide my confusion.
'You're way daft,' and she gentle-punched me.

Fourteen

Mary Ann caught up with me as I went out of the school gate. 'Where are you going?'

I had two pound coins in my pocket. 'To buy fudge.'

'Oh, OK.' She fell into step beside me. We went under the railway bridge and passed Victoria Hall with its posters advertising coming concerts. 'I saw you before.'

I stopped. 'Did you?'

'You were out at the weekend, weren't you, out walking.'

Oh. That wasn't what I'd hoped she'd say.

'You went past ours. With your parents.'

I shook my head. 'I haven't got *parents*.'

Her eyes widened. 'Are you an orphan? I'm half an orphan. My mum died in a car crash.'

'Me too.' I backtracked quickly. 'I mean, I've not got a dad.'

'Who was that then, the man with you?'

'Nobody,' I said fiercely.

'Oh.' She kept quiet then till I'd bought the bag of fudge and offered her a lump. As the crunchy sweetness coated my tongue, I had an idea. I led her to the bank on the corner and pressed my finger in: B-E-

'What are you doing?'

-E-N-I-

That's when it happened again. I was going elsewhere, yet I was in the same place, and this time I didn't feel dizzy at all. And now Mary Ann was with me. The cars that had been parked in the square weren't there. In front of the town hall were carts, creaking and rocking, laden with pigs and sheep, waiting to be unloaded into wooden pens. Horses stamped their great hairy hooves and when they tossed their heads their harness jangled. It was noisy what with that jangling, the stamping of hooves on cobbles, the creak of carts and rumble of wheels and the farmers shouting.

We dodged our way through the pens and the horses just as a boy came running down the steps from the Shambles where sheep and cattle were butchered. He was in such a hurry to get away from a man behind that he tripped and slid down the rest of the steps and fell in a heap at the bottom, dropping the bucket he'd been carrying. Dog turds splattered to the ground. He landed right in them. It was Morphet.

His father was on him again, holding his wrist. He raised his heavy stick. 'Damned brat! Ushelesh turd! I cursh t'day you wash born!'

Morphet cowered away, doubling up, protecting his face. 'I've done nowt, Father, I swear, nowt!'

'Yer wash born. Thash not nowt. An' I cursh tha' day!' The stick landed with a great thwack on his back, where he'd almost no flesh. Through his ragged shirt you could see the knobs of his spine, like teeth, he was so skinny.

'Don't do that!' I charged in front of his father, braver this time. 'He's done nowt. You heard him.'

'Tsk, tsk,' tutted some women who were passing, maybe at

me, maybe at him, I didn't know and didn't care.

'Let Morphet go!' I cried.

He was so surprised that he did. He spat in the road, a glob of spit that wobbled and glistened and then he grabbed me instead, gripping my ear so tightly that I couldn't escape. Out of the corner of my eye I saw Morphet scarper.

'Who the hell are you t' tell me wha' to do?' He twisted my ear; it burned as if a red-hot poker was on it. His breath stank of rotting teeth and his eyes were small and bloodshot.

'Language! Language!' tutted the same women, stopping to watch.

Mary Ann tugged at his sleeve, trying to get him to loosen his hold on me.

But he yanked me across to our shop on the corner. 'Your boy triesh to tell me wha' to do wish my shon,' he slurred.

'He was beating Morphet, Father. Again. For nothing, just for being alive.'

'Aye. Yon lad of thine needs a goo' beating hisself. "Shpare t' rod an' spoil t' child," as the Good Book says.'

I didn't care. '"Whoso shall offend one of these little ones, it were better for him that a millstone were hanged about his neck and that he were drowned,"' I squared up to him and quoted Scripture back as well as I could.

'Bible learner! Lippy sod!' He lunged at me, and missed.

'Will you stop that language!' Father said sternly to him. 'Neighbour, you stink. You cannot speak straight. You've been at Obadiah Baynes' again,' he said, pointing at the drink shop over the way. 'If you listened in chapel instead of snoring, you'd have marked the warnings about drink.'

''S no law 'gainst drink!'

'Maybe not.' Father gave me a push. 'You, go and find your mother. Take Mary Ann with you.'

But Mother had told me to be kind to Morphet. 'We have to help Morphet pick up the turds,' I said to Mary Ann.

'Benjamin! I do not wish to tell you again. I said, inside. Now then, Amos Bibber...'

'But we-'

'Inside!'

I turned to go in but there was no door. I turned so tightly that I made Mary Ann stumble, she was so close. 'Come on, we've got to pick them up. Quick!'

An elderly couple walked past, trailing shopping bags on wheels.

'Pick what up?' Mary Ann asked.

'Don't you see?' I said fiercely. 'Morphet's dad'll murder him one of these days.'

'Who's Morphet?'

'You know.'

'I don't. What are you talking about, P? You went all funny back there.'

'But you were with me.'

She looked blank. She was in her school clothes, as before. So was I. I stared at her. I whirled round, looking for the saddlery. Instead the bank building faced me.

I shook my head to clear it. 'Look, are we ghosts?'

'Ghosts? What are you talking about? You're weird, you are.'

'I'm not.'

'You are. Ghosts? Ha!' And she pinched me.

'Ow! That hurt.'

'So? Do ghosts pinch?'

'No then. Let me pinch you back.'

'No way! I'm a girl. You can't pinch me.' She dodged, giggling.

But I needed to see if my pinches were real too. I pinched myself instead, hard. It hurt all right.

That night in bed, through my eyelids, I saw orange light, growing stronger. I felt warmth on my face. I opened my eyes and saw flames dancing. I was sitting on the fender at the fire in the parlour, with my sister Grace. Mother was knitting in her chair at the other side of the fire. Father was smoking his pipe and reading by the light of a tall candle, just behind us. From the shadows the clock went *clunk, clunk.* Mother's needles clicked and the fire crackled. It was snug in there. I was swinging a length of Mother's green wool at Polly. She crouched, watching the wool swing from side to side, her cat's eyes narrowed at it. She pounced. Too late. I'd moved the wool away. 'Now me,' said Grace, elbowing me aside. 'Give it here,' she said, taking the wool.

'I am concerned, Mr Waugh, about something that I have heard in town,' said Mother to Father. 'It is said that there has been cursing with the evil eye.'

'Base superstition,' said Father, laying his book aside for a moment. 'Cursing does no one good, neither he who curses, nor he who is cursed.'

'Who's been cursing, Mother?' asked Grace.

'Ssh. No matter. Tst, tst, poor Polly, being teased like that,' Mother said, putting aside her knitting and getting to her feet. 'Benjamin, Grace, I shall fetch you both hot milk with liquorice and then you may join the little ones in bed.'

When she brought our small mugs to us, we sat quietly, gazing into the flames. Polly curled up on my leg, warm and soft.

Fifteen

'Zoe,' called out Mr Magnus.

'Good morning, Mr Magnus.'

'Darren.'

'Good morning, Mr Magnus.'

'Kyle.'

'Good morning, Mr Magnus.'

'Daniel.'

'Good morning, Mr Magnus.'

'Percy. Percy!' Mr Magnus repeated. 'I believe it is you that I see over there.'

I only half-heard. I'd gone too far, cursing the gowk. Could my cursing come back to haunt me? I heard giggling and felt a nudge. Daniel was nodding over at Mr Magnus with the register. That brought me back. 'Good morning, Mr Magnus,' I said, and sneezed, all over the table.

'Welcome,' he said, to more laughter, 'and bless you.'

'That's my book you've sneezed on,' hissed Louise.

'Mary Ann,' he called.

'Good morning, Mr Magnus.' She grinned at me, and I sneezed again, three times in quick succession. I had caught cold, probably in the graveyard.

'How many seconds in a year? Quick, quick,' said Mr Magnus. 'How many minutes in a millennium?'

'A million?'

He smiled. 'No, Kyle. It sounds as though it should be that, I agree, but it isn't.'

Kyle scratched his head.

'Think about the question properly. Anyone?'

'A billion?'

'No. Anyone else? Work it out, come on. Yes, you may use your calculators.'

'I'm going camping at the weekend,' I heard Daniel whisper to Mary Ann, their heads close together, so I couldn't catch her eye, talk more to her. Louise was filling in sums, twining hair round her finger. It'd be fun to go camping. I wished I was part of the whispering. I looked back down at my blank sheet of paper and sneezed again. My finger began tracing letters on my page: B-E-N-J-

Figures blurred and jumped on the page. There was a hissing in my ears, and a voice sounding as if from far off. Then the sounds cleared:

'Four tens are forty, three tens are thirty, two tens are twenty.' I was chanting along with the others on my bench. We were meant to be encouraging the little ones on the benches in front with their multiplication tables, but the master had us doing them backwards so as to keep us alert. My woollen trousers and jacket were hot and itchy; the sun was shafting through the high windows right on me and I longed to be up on the moors with the cotton grass nodding their white heads in the breeze and tiny scarlet pimpernel peeping through and the crush of wild thyme beneath my feet, and purple and white clover sweetening the air.

'Six nines are fifty-four, five nines are forty-five...' We were packed as tight as herrings on forms, facing front. Mary Ann and the other girls in their white pinafores were separated from us, on the other side of the aisle. The tall, thin master beat out time as we chanted, walking up and down the rows of benches, banging a stick on the floor as he went.

'Eleven eights are eighty-eight, ten eights are eighty...'

'You coming rabbiting with us after school?' One of my friends nudged me in the side.

'If I don't have to help Father, yes,' I whispered back.

'Benjamin Waugh! Is that you again? Will you stop your jabbering at once!' The master banged the stick extra hard. If I didn't watch out, I'd get it on the palm of my hand or on my shoulder. 'Eyes front!' he called.

'Seven sevens are forty-nine... two sevens are fourteen.'

'Enough!' He went to the board and wrote down the names of countries. 'Geography now, boys and girls. Who can tell me the capital of Sweden?'

'Stockholm, sir.'

'Good. Turkey?'

'Constaninople, sir.'

'Excellent. Bavaria?'

The answers came thick and fast. We all liked geography, and he was good at telling us about the different countries.

From outside music floated through the windows, music that made me want to tap my feet and move.

'Do not be distracted!' He banged his stick down hard once more. 'Let us see whether you can drown out the barrel organ, because I shall not let you out to dance. Eyes front! What is the capital of France? Shout it out, all at once!'

That was easy. 'Paris, sir,' we chorused.

'Austro-Hungary?'

A woman came into the classroom and went over to the master and whispered in his ear. Our chanting faltered.

'Continue! Continue!' He waved his stick at us.

But this one was more difficult. 'Vatican City, sir?' a girl called out at last.

He didn't answer to say whether or not she was right. 'Benjamin Waugh.' He pointed his stick at me.

'I'm delighted to see you come out of your daydream to be with us.' Mr Magnus was looking right at me. 'Can you provide the answer that we're looking for?'

'Er...' I sneezed. Where was Austro-Hungary? 'Berlin, sir?'

'Berlin, sir?' he echoed. 'What kind of answer is that? You're away with the fairies! Louise?'

'One thousand six hundred.'

'Right.'

One thousand six hundred? It wasn't geography at all, it was arithmetic.

'See if you can work out how she got that, Percy.'

I stared round the classroom, at my classmates, boys and girls seated together on chairs around tables, at the white computer screen on one wall and bright posters and paintings and poems on the others. I bent back to my maths book.

Harry was whispering to Tim. They were both glancing at me.

When the bell went, I didn't look up. I didn't rush out with the others. I went on writing until I was the only one left in the classroom.

'Out you go, Percy,' said Mr Magnus from his desk in the corner.

Slowly, I closed my exercise book. Slowly, I pushed back my chair and stood.

'Mr Magnus...'

Mr Magnus' pen paused in mid-air. 'Yes?'

'Please, Mr Magnus. You said I was daydreaming.'

'I did, didn't I. Well, weren't you?'

'I don't know.'

'Now there's an interesting answer.' Mr Magnus pushed back his chair, tugged at his waistcoat, came and perched on my table. 'You don't know?'

'Not really.' I shook my head. 'What is a daydream? I mean, if it's a dream at night, you don't call it a night dream, do you? Unless it's nasty and it's a nightmare. And are the people you see in nightmares ghosts? Or can you daydream at night and have a nightmare in the daytime? Do you dream, Mr Magnus?'

'Whoa. That's a lot of questions. What are you getting at?'

'Do you see people in funny clothes, in the middle of the day, like?'

'In funny clothes? Frequently.'

I flushed. 'I mean, old-fashioned clothes like in the pictures in the corridor.'

'As in, what, nineteenth-century clothes?'

I nodded.

'I can't say that I do, no. Not since Seggleswick had a Victorian fair, at any rate.' He got up from the table, paused, and swung round. 'You are getting on all right, aren't you? You like it here at school, hmm?'

I shrugged, then I nodded.

'Is there something else? Are you sickening for anything apart from this cold of yours?' He felt my forehead.

I hadn't moved. 'Please, Mr Magnus. If you look in a mirror, and you're on your own, can you see anybody except yourself?'

'No, Percy. A mirror is only reflective glass.' He peered down at me more closely. 'And are you getting enough sleep, going to bed on time?'

I nodded again, because it was true; I was going to bed on time. Way before, mostly.

'Good. Now, out with you. I need to get on with my marking.'

I traipsed out. My back tingled. I could sense his eyes on me, watching me go.

They were waiting for me when I got out. 'We're off to play Cherry Arse.' Daniel told me, winking heavily and nudging me in my side. Tim was with him, smirking. Harry was chucking a football from hand to hand, whistling.

'Oh.' I winked heavily and nudged Daniel back.

'Do you know it?' Tim asked, looking as if he was trying not to laugh.

'Yes,' I said. Then I thought better of it; they'd be sure to find me out. 'Well, no, not really.'

'Thought not!' Tim crowed. 'We'll teach you.'

Harry tucked the ball under his arm and we went to where the path ran alongside the fire station and turned in till we were facing the side wall of the building. 'You're goalie,' Tim told me, 'and this,' he led me over to the wall, 'is your goal.' He left me there and went to stand opposite with the other two.

'What, the whole wall?' There were no windows there to break, but it was way too wide for a goal.

Harry kicked the ball. It thudded on the wall an arm's length away. 'One!' he shouted.

'Can't one of you be the keeper?' I was good on wing, not in goal.

Tim ran forward for the ball and kicked it. 'Two!' he shouted, as it hit the wall.

'I'm not ready!' I protested, but the ball had bounced back to Harry and he'd kicked it.

'Three! Four!' then, 'Five!'

'You'd better start saving, P,' Daniel called.

'It's not fair. I was talking.' I had my hands on my hips and I was getting quite cross. 'What is this game anyway?'

'Cherry Arse. We told you. Six! Seven! Guard your goal!'

They were laughing. One more, two more thudded through on to the wall goal.

'And, ten!' shouted Tim, jumping up and down. 'Turn round, bend over.'

'Why?'

'Because you let in ten balls, dumbo. So now we get to kick the ball at you.'

'But you never told me the rules. That's not fair.'

'Just b-bend over, P, g-get it over with,' Harry said.

'Hands on knees,' Tim called.

I turned round, hands on knees.

'Don't look round. You can't, it's against the rules. You first,' I heard Daniel say.

The ball bounced beside me. 'Missed!' I straightened.

'Get back down. My turn,' Daniel called.

'Ow!' The ball hit me fair and square on the bum.

'Stay down, P-P,' called Harry. 'It's me now.'

This time the ball just scraped off and bounced at the side.

I turned to face them. 'Can I come out of goal now?'

'No,' said Tim. 'Now the score goes back to zero. You stay in there till you save a goal.'

I gritted my teeth and faced them. This time, straightaway I saved the first shot and started walking.

'Uh-huh.' Tim waved at me to go back.

'Why?'

'Because you got up between shots.'

'Give over, Tim. Let him out,' said Harry.

'Nah!' and Tim kicked the ball at me. 'He's soft in the head, lying in a coffin. It's evil, that is.'

I caught it again, looked at Harry. 'You told them, too?'

He shrugged.

'Two volleys now and no headers,' Tim shouted.

'No! You keep changing the rules. Daniel?' I appealed.

'I'm off home,' Daniel said in answer. 'You coming, Harry?'

'Ball, P!' Tim ordered.

I kicked it to him, and then the three of them went off. But Daniel clapped me on the shoulder as he went past. 'Pretty cool, P.'

I watched them go. It must have been another test. 'Pretty cool,' Daniel had said. They hadn't asked me to go with them and I wouldn't trail behind them this time. So I waited till they were gone, then I walked up to the square myself. I might buy fudge for Mum.

Sixteen

'You scallywag!' A hand landed on my shoulder. 'I need you,' Father said. 'Where have you been?'

He didn't give me a chance to answer.

'Playing with your friends, I'll be bound.' He answered straight in for me. 'I'm after a side of leather for Mr Procter's new saddle. Good cow's leather. Go and fetch it, there's a good lad. Ask them to put it on account,' he called after me.

I swerved between the groups of leather dealers haggling at the door of the Talbot and went on past King Billy's. A carthorse clumped its way down towards me on Warehouse Hill, a wagonful of straw swaying behind. It left so little room that I ducked out of the way and found myself staring up the snout of a scraped and gutted pig carcass hanging from a hook outside the butcher's. I wriggled on, past the open door to the bakery; warm yeasty, sugary smells wafted out to mix with the steaming manure from a passing farmer's horse. There were fat rascals in the window with a special dusting of sugar on them but when I patted my pocket to see if I had a penny in there, I hadn't, so I stopped gazing and ran on up, dodging ponies and handcarts and shoppers.

But there was Morphet, trudging up the road ahead, lugging

two buckets of dog dung this time, full to the brim and stinking.

'All right, Morphet?'

He halted. He was paler than ever, and there was a gash over his eye. His cheek was purple and swollen.

'Here. Give me them.'

He was almost as surprised to hear me offer as I was myself, and he surrendered the buckets. As he did, a turd rubbed against my hand and plopped to the ground. I pretended not to notice.

But Morphet did. He bent down and scooped it up. He stood again, swaying with exhaustion. 'They're not yours,' he said, 'and you mustn't go dropping any. Father'll skin me alive if he sees you carrying the pails. It's our money in there. Give 'em back.'

'You're all right,' I reassured him, though I did glance up and down the street to make sure that Amos Bibber wasn't anywhere near. 'I'll give you them back when we get there.'

He fell into step beside me, dragging his bare feet. It was easier walking with him because people just got out of our way as they smelled us coming. Where buildings crowded the road and the cobbles were stained a reddish brown, I would have lost my footing in the slime if Morphet hadn't reached out a hand and stopped me in time; his bare feet gripped the matted fur and wool and gristle in the road better than my clogs. 'Give me the pails now,' he begged, 'or you'll lose all the dung.'

I only gave him one. The other I held on to. We climbed the steps to the tannery and handed them to the overseer who tipped them into the pit to join the brown stuff already there. 'In you get.'

Morphet slipped in, up to his knees in watered-down dog and pigeon muck. 'Don't stand about idle, Benjamin Waugh!' the overseer said. 'Do you not want to help with the bating? Take your clogs off. In you go.'

'Father told me to bring back leather.'

'Aye, did he. Well, you can help us a bit first, then I'll let you have the leather. These calf skins need softening for gloves and our bater's off sick. So we need feet to tread.'

'He'll not want to get his feet mucky!' Morphet said, but I saw his sideways look at me.

'I will and all,' I said, and got in. The two of us trampled the leather. The dung was warm and claggy against my feet and legs. Bits splashed up on my breeches as I trod on the skins below, walking up and down.

But Father would be wondering where I'd got to. 'Can I get out now?'

'Chicken!' Morphet jeered.

I gave him a shove. 'That's not fair. Father doesn't like to be kept waiting when he's busy.'

Morphet toppled and only just stopped himself from falling right in the smelly stuff.

'Aye. Well, mebbe next time you'll stay longer,' said the overseer. 'I'll give your coin to Morphet this time.'

Morphet didn't catch my eye as I laced up my boots and took the roll of leather the overseer gave me. I hefted it on my shoulder and walked quickly back down the road.

'What kept you? Oh, don't tell me. You've been at that pit.' In the shop Father took the leather from me. 'No harm done. You'll need to understand the processes involved for when you take over the business. It's good to get stuck in.'

Mother came through and overheard him. 'He'll not be a saddler,' she said to herself, looking through me. 'He'll be brain-learning.' Then she snapped free. 'Outside with you! Out!' She chased me on to the street, brought out a bucket and began scrubbing me clean at the door.

'You've forgotten his ears, missus!' People were gathering to watch. So was Mary Ann, and she, like them, was laughing at me.

'Hold still,' Mother said as I squirmed to get away. But she let me go soon after that and went indoors.

'My mother sent you this,' Mary Ann handed me a cabbage, giggling, 'now you're clean. We've got that many cabbages, we thought your mother would like one. Will you give it to her? And hurry: there's a bear! I'll wait.'

I raced through to the kitchen with it, and stopped. 'Mother? Are you sickening?' She was sitting with her head thrown back and her hand on her breast. It wasn't like her just to sit, not to be moving about doing things. John was playing at her feet with a peg doll and Jane was on a stool at the sink, peeling potatoes.

'I am just a little tired,' she answered, rallying. 'My feet are so swollen, I was resting them. Come over here. Stand before me.' I dumped the cabbage on the draining board. She rested her arms on mine and looked searchingly at me. 'Will you always be a good boy, our Benjamin?'

I fidgeted. 'Can I go and see the bear? Only Mary Ann's waiting for me outside. The cabbage is from her mother.'

'In a moment.' She went on surveying me, her face serious. 'Will you remember always that God is a loving God, and so should you be loving?' she went on. 'Will you always do your best to help those less fortunate than yourself?'

'Like saving pennies for the poor?'

She nodded.

'Like helping Morphet bate the leather?'

She smiled faintly. 'Very well, like that too, yes. Seek justice when you see injustice done. And remember to say your prayers.'

'Yes, Mother.' I squirmed, wanting to be off. Why was she was being so serious? It wasn't even Sunday. 'May I go now?'

She sighed. 'Very well. Take Jane with you.'

By the time Jane had washed and dried her hands and put on a clean pinafore and slipped one hand in mine and one in Mary Ann's outside, it was easy to see where the bear was from the crowd already gathered beyond the town hall. Grace was there already close to the Shambles with its smell of fresh meat, and she waved us over.

The bear on all fours looked like an enormous sad dog; its fur was matted and worn away in patches. There was a chain round its neck which was held at the other end by a man in a suit of clothes as dull and threadbare as his animal.

'Dance! Dance!' we chanted.

'Or don't it know how to?' jeered a horseman.

In answer, the bear's handler jerked on the chain round the creature's muzzle, while a second man took out a fiddle and started playing a jig. The bear's head swivelled round, and at the next tug of the chain, it lumbered to its feet.

We fell back. It was huge. It didn't look like a dog now! Even the handler only came up to its forepaws which it waved in the air as it shambled first one way then the other. Its eyes glared dully round at us.

'You,' the handler called to John, giving him his cap, 'take this round for me.'

'Penny for the bear!' John sang. 'Ha'pence for the bear! Farthing for the bear!' One or two people put money in, but most drew back, or wandered off, not wanting to pay.

Then Morphet was there, a gleam in his eye. 'Give over.' He grabbed the cap. 'I'll get 'em to pay.' He stuck the cap right under people's noses: 'Penny! Penny! Ha'penny!' He was so close they had to fork out. Besides, you could see them wanting rid of him and his stench. By the time he came to where we were standing, he had quite a few coins. 'Ha'penny!' he ordered a woman beside us. She fumbled in the thick folds of her skirt and dropped in a coin. As he turned, I saw him grab the ha'penny from the cap and stick it in his pocket. He rubbed his nose on his sleeve so as to hide what he'd done. 'See? That's how to get 'em to pay,' he told John, handing the cap back.

'Mister, hey, mister,' one lad shouted, 'Let it off the chain, will you?'

'D'you want to be mauled?'

'Mauled by them claws? Don't make me laugh,' he said, greatly daring. I wouldn't want to be grabbed by them; even if they had been blunted, they were still as long as my thumb.

I don't know who tired first, the bear or the violinist, but suddenly the animal was back on all fours. One of my friends darted forward and jabbed a stick in the bear's side.

It reared up, batting with its hands. The handler roared at it to stop and then he roared at us to flit!

We scattered, laughing. 'Wait for me!' cried Jane.

'Can you get me summat to eat?' I heard Morphet cry as we ran.

'Where are you?' I called.

There was no Morphet. Jane had vanished too and so had the pony carts and a man on horseback and the bear and I was standing there in the market place between two parked cars.

'Have you lost someone, love?' asked a woman unlocking the door to her car.

'Yes. I mean, no, not really,' I answered, a hollow feeling in my stomach.

She peered at me. 'Are you sure? You look a bit dazed.'

I turned to go, looking back at the cars all the time, wanting them to be transformed back into a bear and handler and the small crowd, looking for Mary Ann and for Jane and Grace and Morphet. And seeing none of them. Everything looked sharper than usual, as if in a photograph and not real life.

There was a shout behind me and my head swung round; it was only someone hailing a friend. But in that second of pausing and turning my head, I caught a reflection. In the glass of the bakery window, I saw myself. Behind me was the reflection of another boy – who looked like me. He was right on my heels, touching me. Behind him, was yet another figure, taller and heavier, with what looked like a bushy beard jutting from his chin, as if he was me and the other boy, only older. We were like playing cards in a pack when you fan them out.

In the window they were so close behind, you'd have thought I'd feel their breath on my neck, but I felt nothing. I glanced over my shoulder to make quite sure there really was no one, no lad, no man, right behind me.

There was no one. I'd only glanced away for a second. Now when I looked back, the window showed only one reflection, mine. There I stood, alone, staring into it.

Seventeen

That night I waited till Mum and the gowk were in bed before slipping out of the door to go back towards the graveyard. Luckily, I'd stopped sneezing. But I never reached the graveyard.

'Race you to the market, our Benjamin!' The voice was right in my ear. A bunch of us were tearing down the high-walled ginnel, dark in the shade of the sun. I heard panting behind as we crossed the river, and knew that Mary Ann was trying to catch up but she wasn't as fast as we were because of not wearing breeches. She drew level when we stopped at the apple tree where its branches hung over a garden wall. We jumped and grabbed the fruit, one, two, each, and into our pockets, and then ran, laughing, till we stopped short. Two men were in our path in rough, dirty clothes. One, his hair all matted, was swaying drunkenly and singing:

'In eighteen hundred and forty-four
    I landed on the Liverpool shore;
Me belly was empty, me hands were sore
    With working on the railway, the railway.
I'm weary of the railway…'

'Weeee-aaar-y of t' raaaiillway!' echoed the other man, bellowing, swaying behind him, mocking him. Morphet's father!

The navvy took a long swig from the bottle that swung from his hand. Brown liquid drooled down his chin. Morphet's father grabbed at the bottle, but the navvy didn't let go. They swayed together then fell down. Morphet must have been lurking in the shrubs watching because he darted out and tried to get his father to his feet, but his father knocked him away. Morphet caught sight of us, standing there in a group, and scowled. I threw him an apple. It thudded to the ground. He grabbed it, and scarpered.

Slowly the navvy got to his feet and looked round, his eyes all red and blurred. He lurched towards us. 'Hey, you, give's a penny.' Foul alcoholic fumes billowed towards us as he stretched out a claw of a hand. We backed off, shaking our heads. As a woman approached, basket over her arm, covered with a checked cloth over her arm, he reeled over to her instead. 'Oy, spare us a penny, lady.' He knuckled his forehead. But that made him lose his footing and he tumbled back on the path, where Morphet's father was still lying, singing away to himself, 'On t' raaaaiiilwaaaay.'

The woman shuddered and continued on her way. 'Scum,' she muttered as her skirts swished past, coming close to us to avoid the navvy. He was half-sprawled over Morphet's father and they were singing together. A rumble like thunder rolled towards us. I looked up at the sky, just as the rumbling turned to a roar and I was standing under a railway bridge and a train pounded overhead. A solitary streetlight lit up mist that billowed in clouds around. All was still. There was no drunk navvy or farmer's wife. No Morphet's father or Morphet. No friends, no Mary Ann. Just me, in my pyjamas, and the train.

I ran back the way I had come but this time the pebbly muddy track was a road and the ginnel was lit. Mist swirled about me and clung to my hair and jumper. I breathed in damp as I ran, on and on till I reached the steps and ran up them, panting. The light went on in their bedroom. I heard the door to the bathroom open and close. I shut my door, kicked off my slippers and leapt into bed.

There were footsteps on the landing. My door opened. The light clicked on.

'Percival? I thought I'd heard odd noises in here.' The gowk picked up a slipper. 'This is soaking wet.' He came closer. 'Why are you wearing a jumper?'

I didn't answer. I was listening to another sound. Mum was throwing up again. She shouldn't be sick. He should be. It was him I'd cursed.

His eyes fell on the outside door. He went over to it. In my hurry, I hadn't shut the bolts. He tried the handle, and the door opened. 'Percival? This door was locked.'

'What's up?' Mum was in the doorway now. 'Why are you waking Percy up, Ian?'

'He was awake already. He's been wandering about outside. Somehow he's opened that door. Sweetheart, get back into bed.' He steered her away. 'I'll sort this out.'

I heard him go downstairs. In no time he was back with the key. Grimly he locked the door and shot home the bolts. 'This key will be kept somewhere else now. I'm not having you opening that door again, do you hear?'

Eighteen

'This tea's lukewarm,' the gowk complained. 'Boil us some water, would you? And hurry; I don't want to be late for that drink with my colleagues, I must get away on time,' he said in one breath. He prodded the crumpet on his plate.

I examined him for signs of sickness. He looked as healthy as ever.

'Any chance of another of these?' he asked.

I rolled my eyes at Mum.

'What's the matter with it?' Mum asked.

'It's not a crumpet, it's toast!' He bucked with laughter.

'It's a bit crisp round the edges, that's all. Fusspot! Anyway, aren't you in a hurry?' But she kissed the top of his head and put another under the grill.

I finished spreading butter over my own crumpet, watching it leak down into the holes and then sloshed Mum's blackcurrant jam on top and took small bites of it, partly so as to make it last, but also so I could stay there while Mum cleared away after he'd gone. She came back to the table and, resting her elbows on it, pressed her thumbs into the side of her eyes, closing them, and sighed. When she opened her eyes, she saw me watching her. 'Bit of a headache.' She smiled.

'Mum, can dreams be real?'

'Hmm. What's real?' She propped her head in her chin and stared out of the window.

'Mum? Mum?'

'Oh, go and play. Make something with your Lego. You've not touched it for days.'

I chewed my lip. 'He'll clear it away.'

'He won't. We've talked about it and he's agreed that you can keep it out. In a tidy fashion, mind.'

And when I went through, I saw that he'd marked off a corner of the room. BUILDING SPACE he'd written on a card in front of it. I took out the chassis and did start building again. But I wasn't sure I could really trust him to leave it afterwards. It made it difficult to concentrate on finding the right pieces in the right order.

'Your mother and I are going to the pub for a drink. We've got things to discuss.' He was back. 'We shan't be long.'

'Can I go to Mary Ann's?'

'Is she a friend of yours?' Mum asked, brightening. 'Tell you what. Why don't you ring this Mary Ann and ask her over?'

Because I hadn't got her phone number, but he butted in anyway. 'I don't think we want hordes of children around the place, messing it up.'

She glanced at him. 'We'll talk about it later,' she said to me.

'Can I watch TV then?'

'No. I've told you before.' He was getting irritated. 'You're not to go into our bedroom. It's our private space. You have yours, we have ours.'

'Can't I move the TV into another room?'

'Enough. No is no. I'm sure you can find something to do.

No touching my CD player or my laptop either. Anyway, I thought you were busy making your log loader. Why don't you get on with that? Don't make a mess!' Behind his back, I saw Mum frowning to herself. She hugged me hard, and they were gone.

I cheated. The minute they were safely out of the gate, I went up to their bedroom. At least that wasn't locked. And, as luck would have it, by lying on my tummy in the doorway and stretching as far as I could, I could reach the remote on the carpet.

The set was turned partly towards me. I pressed it on and upped the volume from where I sat on the floor in the doorway. There was a programme on river monsters, giant fish from the deep which would gnaw off a man's arm as soon as look at him, snakes with scales as big as my hand, an eel which eats men whole. I was way into the programme, when the front door downstairs shut.

Quickly I pressed the remote to off. I threw it into the room to where it had been, almost. I got up and closed the door.

He was coming up the stairs. He went into the bedroom and sniffed, then ran his hand over the television set as I watched.

It'd be warm! I hadn't thought of that.

He raised his eyebrows at me. 'Have you been in here?'

I shook my head.

'Are you sure?'

Again I shook my head. I hadn't, had I.

'I think you're lying. Go to your room.' His voice was shaking. 'You can come down when supper's on the table.'

It wasn't fair! I hadn't actually been in his bedroom!

I flung myself on my bed, and wished myself away. I wished

myself anywhere but here. My thoughts skittered all over the place. What was he telling Mum now, downstairs? I bet she wouldn't have been cross. I wish I had brothers and sisters. Daniel, Harry, Tim, they all had. Even Mary Ann; she said she had a brother. I had a brother and sisters, and proper parents - somewhere else. I couldn't lie still for thinking. I tossed and turned, I tried curling up, I tried lying on my back, nothing was right.

'Pray sit down, you tinker! Sit down and sit still. Anyone would think you had thorns in your pants, always leaping about!'

'Or fleas.' John nudged me. 'Oh, keep away, keep away!'

Jane giggled behind her hand.

'Children, children. A little more peace and respect at table, if you please.'

'Yes, Father. I'm sorry, Father.'

His stern face didn't relax into a smile, but nor did his eyes flash fury at us either. 'Has your mother baked a special cake for your birthday, young John, I wonder?'

Mother didn't stir. John looked worried. There was no cake on the table. His gaze wandered round the room. Both candles on the mantelpiece were lit and, because of his birthday, the candles in the wall sconces, too. The windowsill beneath the small window was in shadow but the oak dresser and side table were visible in the candlelight and there was no cake there either.

Mother's mouth twitched.

I shoved back my chair and jumped to my feet.

'I'll fetch it.' Grace was getting up in her usual quiet way.

'Sit down, Benjamin. And you, Grace,' said Mother. 'Jane helped me make the cake, so let Jane fetch it in. She can manage.'

Jane went to the kitchen, and returned, bearing a sponge cake with lighted candles. 'We iced it specially, our John,' she said, 'and look, four candles.'

As she set it down before him, we sang our birthday song to John, Father conducting us with a spoon:

'God be with you protecting,
The Lord be with you directing,
The Spirit be with you strengthening,
For ever and for evermore.'

'Blow, John, blow!' we shouted.

He stood and managed to blow out all four candles in one.

It felt good there in the flickering firelight and candlelight, all together. We took it in turn to tell a story, first Father then Mother but she didn't finish hers because she said she was weary, so then it was my turn.

I told them about a barefoot boy who never had a birthday tea, a barefoot boy who was beaten, whose face was scratched and bloodied. About how he was rescued by an elephant, an elephant which hauled the boy out with his trunk, an elephant left behind from years and years and years ago when the moors were wooded and warmer...

Nineteen

Gone to doctor's. Sandwich in bag. Back soon. Be good,
   Love, Mum

The gowk must have told her to lock up, because I couldn't get in. I went up to the outside door of my bedroom just in case, but that was no good either. I wasn't really surprised. I took the sandwich she'd left hanging in a bag from the door handle, shoved it in my pocket and set off up the hill.

At the first gate I took out the sandwich and bit in. What about Mum being sick, and her headaches? She couldn't be very sick or she'd be stopping in bed, the way I had in the spring when I'd had flu. Then a picture came into my head, of Morphet at the sink and Mother – Father had said she was expecting.

Mum had been sick in the early hours of the morning. What if she was pregnant, too? I choked on my mouthful. Morning sickness. She could be. Maybe that was why she'd gone to the doctor. I crossed a field, chewing squashed bread and cheese, not really tasting it. If Mum was pregnant we'd be stuck here for ever and ever. A cow, somewhere out of sight, groaned hoarsely. Shaggy horned cattle clustered about my side of the kissing gate. They just gazed through their thick fringes at me when I shouted at them to let me through, but as I came through the gate, they did lumber away. There, against the wall was the cow, howling. She was standing over a calf, not moving, dead; flies were dancing on its open eyes.

I ran from the mother cow's mourning, across that moor and along and up two stone steps of a stile in the wall. I wanted brothers and sisters, but not from the gowk! I had to get back and check on Mum.

I was about to jump off the stile when something made me halt and turn back and look. Except, I couldn't see properly. A haze was creeping over my eyes, blurring things.

Something white shimmered in the grass, and the blurring cleared. I jumped down and raced for the mushroom, but brother John was there first. I let him take it. Grace was ahead with the basket, crouching down picking other field mushrooms. They glowed against the green grass and blue-grey thistles and brown cowpats, and we moved among bulls and cows and calves, careful not to get between a mother and her young. John helped fill Grace's basket; I took off my jumper and used that. When we'd filled basket and jumper, we clambered up the slope and lay down, our heads propped against tufty grass and stones half-covered in moss. We passed bread to each other, tearing off bits and munching. A bird wheeled overhead, a skylark, singing its dipping, swaying song. When I closed my eyes it was as though Mother was singing over us.

Then my feet were taking me to the kitchen in a house that was all modern inside, one room leading to another downstairs and no doors. Mum was just sitting, with her feet up, her eyes closed, her head on the gowk's shoulder. He had his arm round her.

'Am I a ghost or something?' I asked her. I mean, how had I got back without knowing? I must have been moving on automatic pilot.

The man goggled at me.

'You, my numkin? Of course you aren't a ghost.' She took her legs off the stool and sat up. 'I should know. Didn't I give birth to you? Come here.' She brushed grass off me. I looked hard at her tummy. 'Lord only knows what you've been up to before coming home; you could do with a bath.'

I grinned, relieved that her tummy looked the same as before. I handed my bundle of jumper to her. 'Look.'

She opened it. 'Mushrooms! You've been picking them - oh, that's grand. We'll have them with our meal.' And she got up and placed a pan on the stove.

'What straight off the moor, grown among cow dirt and sheep droppings?' He was appalled.

She laughed. 'We shan't be eating cow pats! The mushrooms are clean enough. You only have to trim the stalks and knock off bits of old grass. They're good for you. Full of vitamins and minerals.'

'Which?' He questioned.

'Er....' Mum hesitated.

'Potassium,' I said quickly. I was making it up, but Mum had asked me to try so I was and it sounded right.

'And they're *very* low in calories.' Mum winked at me, and got on with cooking them her special way. They smelled great.

'They might be poisonous.' As we sat at the table, he

prodded one with his fork. 'Percival could be attempting to poison me. Poison us, I mean.'

'Ian!' Mum was shocked.

'Joke, poppikins. Just my little joke. A man may have his jokes, I suppose.'

I ignored them both and got on with eating the mushrooms on my plate.

He only had one. 'I'm not at all sure that I trust these.'

'Don't throw them away!' Mum was about to scrape what was left on his plate into the bin. 'I'll take them to Morphet.'

'It's not easy, carrying cooked mushrooms around; you'd better drain them first,' Mum commented. Then she looked up. 'Who's Morphet? Is that a friend of yours?'

I hadn't realised I'd spoken his name out loud. 'Yes.' I ducked my head.

I put them in a plastic bag to take them to school next day. It was daft, but maybe I'd see Morphet somewhere and I could give him them.

Twenty

'Right. Let's recap on the twelve Labours of Hercules. Which were they? The final labour of Hercules. Who can tell me? What does Hercules have to do next? Yes- Harry?'

'He has to g-go to Hades.' He grinned across at me and stuck his thumb up.

'Good. Right. Can anyone tell me another name for Hades?'

Daniel's hand shot up. 'The Underworld?'

'Now there's an interesting thing. The *Underworld*. What do *we* believe in after death?'

'Heaven and Hell,' said Mary Ann.

'Which are?' Mr Magnus gestured. 'Up to Heaven,' and then he pointed down, 'and down to Hell, whereas the ancient Greeks believed that everyone went down, to the Underworld. But the Underworld had different parts to it.'

Hell: on the headstones in the graveyard Hell was never mentioned. That cheered me. I couldn't imagine the gowk going to Heaven, so he couldn't be buried in my graveyard and it wouldn't be spoilt.

'Hey, in that coffin, with Harry, did you lie all the way down in it, I mean with your head and all?' Mary Ann was nudging me.

I flushed. 'Um. Yeh.'

'Did you go to sleep in it?' She looked impressed.

'Of course not. I...'

'Are you two listening?'

'Sorry, Mr Magnus.'

'Now that you know about Hercules and the guard dog Cerberus, you can write your own story,' said Mr Magnus. 'You can pretend you're going to Hades, you can create your own underworld. You can be noble as Hercules, or you can be ignoble. Use the characters from Greek myths, or make up your own. It's up to you. Just use this myth as inspiration.'

I sucked the end of my pen, thinking about graves and curses. About myths and ghosts.

'And, Darren: no machine guns, no motorbikes, no aliens.'

I was already writing:

> One day they were out walking, the young man, his mum, and the man they had to live with. The man walked ahead, planting walking poles in the ground as he went, his head upright. 'Just breathe in that good air,' he told them. 'Stop and take deep breaths.'
>
> The young man, whose name was Ben, obeyed. But when he breathed in, he didn't smell good air. He scrunched up his nose because what he could smell was things rotting.
>
> 'Come along.'
>
> They followed in the man's wake. The stench was getting worse. No one noticed, except for Ben. He had a plan. He gave...

'Round off your sentence, and take it home to finish.'

…no warning.

Twenty-one

I hung around after school with Harry, heading a ball, seeing how long we could keep it in the air, and Mary Ann was with us; she wasn't bad at it, though not as good as I was.

'Shall we do homework together?' asked Mary Ann when Harry sloped off. 'We could go to yours.'

I couldn't exactly tell her she wouldn't be welcome there. 'I've got a better idea.'

She walked with me, over the footbridge and on to the church. 'To the graveyard?' She was surprised. 'So can I see the coffin?'

I pretended not to hear. 'Here's good.' I sat on a grave near the lych-gate. It was like a table up on four sturdy legs, and the stone was warm from the afternoon sun. I sat on one end.

'Cool.' She got down, crosslegged, at the other end. 'Won't the people underneath mind?'

'Course not.' I squinted at the names. 'I expect the Browns would like company.' I took out the paper bag and put it down.

'What's in there?'

'Mushrooms. I picked some yesterday.'

'Bit squashed, aren't they.'

'He won't mind that.'

'Who won't?' But she was laying her books out and didn't seem too bothered when I didn't answer. I wanted to go on with the story that we'd started in class. I opened the book and went on writing from where I'd left off:

> But Ben had a plan. He gave no warning. He'd keep his mum outside and he'd herd the man into the cave and the dark pit. He'd seen how sheepdogs did it. Like a sheepdog, he walked to the side of the man, then to his back, then to the side again.
>
> The man didn't know that Ben was herding him closer and closer to that pit, the pit with the terrible smells. The pit that led to the Underworld, the pit that led to Hell.
>
> They were nearly at the cave.

'Look at you writing, P! We're meant to be doing timetables, aren't we? Can I see?'

I curved my arm round the paper to hide it. 'Maybe later.'

But she was alert now. 'You never said who the mushrooms are for.'

'Someone,' I muttered.

'Huh. You're crazy, you are.' But her eyes were shining as she looked around. She got up from the tomb.

'Where are you going?'

'To look for that coffin. If you won't show me, I'll have to find it myself, won't I.' She stretched and smiled. 'I like it here. It feels almost homey.'

Well it would feel homey for her, wouldn't it. 'That's because you're buried here.' I slammed my hand in front of my mouth. But the words were out and she had heard them and was staring at me, her mouth open.

'I'll show you.' I had to now.

'The coffin, you mean?'

I nodded quickly. I led her to the end of the church, in the shadow of the tower. We went quickly past the Spencer grave and on to the coffin nearby. 'Here. This is where I lay.'

She gazed down at it, and back at me, her eyes wide. 'Wow, P.' She looked round. 'But, what you said about me being buried, um… I don't understand. Do you mean in here? Were you being funny?'

It was no good; I'd have to explain. I turned to the Spencer grave and rested one hand on the headstone. 'There. See?' I pointed to the words: Mary Ann Spencer, died 26th Dec. 1854 aged 15 years.

I watched her like a hawk to see if she changed into the other Mary Ann. She might do. Like the mushrooms had done.

But she didn't. She stood stock-still, reading the long list of dead Spencer children, biting her bottom lip. 'That's so sad.'

'Don't you see? "Mary Ann." It's you!'

'Me?' She looked at me then back at the gravestone, frowning. 'Don't be daft. How can it be me? I'm here, aren't I?'

'It *is* you. I've seen you here before.' I pressed hard into the stone, stared at her name there, and fixed her with my eyes, willing her to see herself in the past.

'You're daft; just because I've got the same name doesn't mean it's me. I've never even been here before. Or inside this church. On Sundays we go to chapel. You know, up beyond the Folly.' She shivered. 'Let's go back to where we were; it's warmer there.'

'The place like a square house with the squiggly iron gate,

up the top road?' I knew it. I'd been past it with Morphet. I'd been inside, too.

'My dad keeps a key and looks after it.'

'What?' I was miles away.

'P? Don't fall asleep? P?'

I only dimly heard her. The sun was warm on my face and my arms and legs seemed to be sinking into the stone and what I was really hearing was singing, and then I was in the chapel and I was singing too, '…my shepherd, I'll not want.' John was piping the words beside me, but Father's voice, coming from the other side of Jane and Grace, was so loud and lusty that it almost drowned out ours. Mr Nelson scratched and swooped on his bass fiddle in the front, leading us in the tune. Slender iron columns painted shiny white held up a gallery and soared up beyond to the ceiling which was blue, as blue as heaven. As I sang, I imagined stars up there, thousands of them, millions, as if it was the night sky.

There was a draught of air as the door at the back of the chapel opened. I twisted round. Ma Cox appeared in the opening and she had Morphet with her, held tightly by his arm. Her mouth was set in the same short, tight line as when I'd delivered coal. She shook Morphet to get him to sit down.

'Sit,' Father whispered to all of us, too. The preacher was climbing the steps to the pulpit. 'I should be obliged if you would turn round, Benjamin.' I had caught sight of Mary Ann with her parents and, as I did so, gave a small wave. 'Benjamin,' warned Father, and 'that's better. Now then. Let's see how this one does,' he muttered, 'whether he is any improvement on the last three.'

'My text for today,' intoned the preacher, 'is "Suffer the little children to come unto me, and forbid them not".'

John glanced up at me. 'That's us,' he said with a wide smile.

'Then you'd best listen, hadn't you.' I winked at him.

'Man was set on this earth to work. "In the sweat of thy face shalt thou eat bread…. The times are hard, but there is hope, in parliament, in the country. Mills are opening once more. There is work anew…'

I settled down and tried to concentrate. Mr Nelson came and sat at the end of our pew and we all squeezed up. My eyes were caught by the wide herringbone pattern of his trousers, the zigs and the zags, as the preacher's words fell about me.

'…too little, too late. I say again, there is work. For those as want it… money in their pockets… but the feckless and lazy set their children to work, and what do they do with the miserable pence their children earn? Go straight to the beer house, spend it and the children go hungry. Did Our Lord mean for children to go to him because their father drank his wages and theirs? He did not!'

He thumped the edge of the pulpit, and I jumped.

'There are beer houses here, yea, in this very town. We can all name them. They are the resort of individuals of depraved, abandoned and desperate character.'

Amos Bibber, Welly Cox. I twisted round to catch Morphet's eye. Father glared at me to turn back.

I wriggled my toes inside my boots to keep awake and listen, but I was squashed in so tightly in the pew and the pot-bellied stove at the end of our pew was belting out heat in waves and the preacher's voice made my eyes slip closed, and my head dropped.

'Didn't you hear what I said?'

Mary Ann was shaking me. 'Wake up, P. You went right off to sleep.'

I blinked at her. 'What did I look like?'

'Like that. Like a boy asleep. Hey, what time have you got for the Glasgow train, the one leaving Edinburgh at 17:40? What did you get for it? P? Aargh!' Mary Ann scrambled off the tomb and we both went running after her book as a sudden squall of wind blew it off.

'Here.' I handed it to her. 'There's a storm coming. Look at the clouds!'

Clouds had covered the sun and the tree tops were swaying. Mary Ann pulled up her collar and gathered her books. 'It's getting cold; there's a storm coming. I'm off home. See you later!' She stuffed them in her bag and ran off, up the hill and out of sight.

A raindrop plopped on to my work and spread out on the page. And another. I gathered up my books, too, and looked for the bag of mushrooms. I couldn't see them. I got down on hands and knees and hunted round the tomb. They were gone. Maybe Mary Ann had taken them. Or the wind might have blown them away. Or, could it have been…?

'Morphet?' I called into the air.

A squall of wind shrieked round me in answer.

Twenty-two

Mary Ann was gone, the mushrooms were gone; even the yew trees bowed as if they were pushing me away. By the time I reached to the house, the wind was howling. The front door was locked. I tried the back door and windows just in case. It was no good, the house was well sealed and there was not even a note from Mum on the door. I looked all round the front doorstep in case one had come unstuck and was lying on the gravel, but there was nothing. I stood on a stone and peered in through the window. It was tidy; so tidy you'd think no one lived there. There was no clue as to where Mum was. I wanted my jacket but it was in there. I wiped my nose and pulled up the collar of my shirt. Maybe she was at the shops and would be back shortly. The neighbour's shed door rattled in the wind. There was nowhere to shelter here.

Torn-off bits of black rubbish bags blew about in the tree beside the graveyard gate as I went back the way I'd come. But when I got closer I saw that they were crows. I turned my back on them and headed for the post-office café, the only place nearby with any sign of life. I fingered a pound coin in my pocket.

Up two steps and in I went. The bell at the top of the door

jangled. There was a wooden counter on my left, shiny from years of polish.

'What are you after, eh? You'll catch a fly if you don't watch out.'

I shut my mouth. I'd been so busy gazing at the shelves reaching to the ceiling full of sweets in big glass jars, that I hadn't noticed the shopkeeper behind the counter.

'Sour peaches, is that what you'd like?'

'I've only got a pound.' I held it up.

'That's plenty for a hundred grams. Or how about Vimto?' He turned to take down a jar. 'They're popular.'

There was a fire on the other side in an old black range, even though it was still only September. The gowk said fires were dirty because they caused dust. Three tables were squashed round the range.

'Which do you want? Or something else?'

What I wanted was to sit there by the bright, leaping flames. I shifted from foot to foot. I wasn't sure how to ask. 'Could I-'

'Could you what?' He turned. 'Oh, I see. Do you want to stop in?'

I nodded.

'All right, no harm. Tables are free. You can. You give me your pound, and how about I give you a ginger beer and a hot muffin and butter. Deal?'

I nodded. 'Thank you.'

I sat on the settle at the side of the black range with its blazing fire. I bit into the muffin when it came, watching the road outside all the time, past the flowers in the window box, bending in the wind. There wasn't much traffic this end of town. Either Mum would come walking past, from the shops, if that was where she'd gone, or I'd see the car drive by. Melted butter dribbled down my chin; I caught it on my finger and licked it clean.

There was the sound of running feet and of laughter outside and the door to the café jangled open. A couple tumbled in. 'Good afternoon. Goodness, it's blowing up out there. The weather's turning. We need some milk, please. And are those really mint humbugs?' I recognised the voice; it was the woman from the graveyard. She had on jeans and sweatshirt and a red scarf tied round her hair; at least, you could see it was meant to be red but, like her jeans and shirt, it was thick with dust, and there were smudges on her cheek and the tip of her nose. 'It's thirsty work, clearing out old rooms,' she confided to the shopkeeper. 'Hi,' she said, noticing me.

I half-raised my hand and sort of said 'Hi' back, but it came out as a bit of a shy mumble. 'May we have a handful of the humbugs?' she asked the shopkeeper.

'Moving here, are you?' He weighed out the sweets.

'Uh-huh. I'm Liz. Hello.'

'And I'm Thomas.' The man at her side held out a hand. 'I'll take the milk.'

Liz gave me a huge, happy smile as they blew out with the same energy they'd come in: 'Bye.'

I felt restless after that. Mum hadn't gone past, nor the car. I'd long finished my muffin and ginger beer and it had stopped raining and the fire was too hot. Four people were at the counter waiting to be served and another two came in behind them. I squeezed past and out of the door, and perched on a bench at the roadside to wait. Dark clouds swirled above my head; the air was still one moment; the next, the trees were bending in the squalls.

Still no Mum. It was boring just sitting there, waiting. Across the way was a rough track I'd not noticed before. As I got up to investigate, the rain started up again. The track led to a huddle of buildings round a courtyard, sunken and hidden from sight. No one was about. There was a big barn door. I crossed the yard, avoiding the bumps and dips in its rough surface, and saw that there was a padlock, but it hadn't been closed. I pushed down the handle and looked in, expecting to see a car.

It wasn't a garage. I stepped over a stone lintel on to a flagged floor, uneven and filthy with age. My hand brushed against the wall, and stones and old plaster crumbled against it. There was an opening on the left but in the dim light I couldn't see how far back it went. My head blundered into a cobweb, hanging from an iron hook in a beam above my head. I clutched the cobweb and tore it off me. The blocks of black slate behind the beam looked mighty and heavy, as if they were pressing down on me. I looked away quickly, to where dim light filtered through from the further end of the passage and crept towards that. At the far end was a lower chamber with a window set in the wall, half-obscured on the outside by ivy. I stood on tiptoe and stretched my arm into the tiny opening that led to the window but it went so far back that I couldn't reach the glass to see what was on the other side.

If only there was a chair or a stool or a block of wood, something to stand on. I stamped my foot in frustration. The stone below me rocked, and I almost overbalanced.

I stamped my foot again.

There – the slab did move! I knelt to examine it. It was

smaller than the others. I pushed it with my fist to see what would happen. It shifted. I leaned all my weight on my fist and it tilted just high enough to get my fingers underneath.

It stank.

I got my fingers out just before it fell shut.

I made it rock up again, a couple of centimetres this time, enough to bend down and peer underneath. The smell was of rotting food, of sweat, of something worse. There was what looked like a hole below. If only there was something to help me raise the slab. I searched the floor. I prowled round the walls. Half hidden in a gap between two stones was a screwdriver which felt sturdy enough when I weighed it in my hand.

I got back on my knees and prised open the stone as before, taking all the weight on my left hand. This time I managed to keep the stone open a crack even though my fingers were shaking from the strain, and I slid in the screwdriver, almost to its handle. But the stone was so heavy it made me dizzy. I thought I'd faint. I sat down quickly. The screwdriver rolled away. The cellar was darkening.

I heard rustling.

I rolled my eyes from side to side, in case there was a mouse. Or a rat. Rain burst outside. It beat on the tiny window. The rustling sounded like whispers and the whispers grew louder. 'Open the trapdoor! You can't...!'

I screamed.

Twenty-three

Footsteps crossed the floor above my head. A door opened. The tapping of shoes coming down and into the yard.

I backed away from the slab, keeping my eyes on it, shaking. I didn't know which was more scary, those whispers, or having to explain why I was trespassing. I wish I hadn't screamed.

The light from the door that I'd come in faded as someone blocked it and moved towards me.

There was only one way out. I whirled round and ran, head down, and cannoned into something soft.

'Ouch!' said a woman's voice. 'Mind out!' Hands took me by the shoulders, but I slipped from her grip and shot off.

'Wait!' she cried as I pelted across the yard, into another shower of rain. 'Wait!' but I was gone, up and along the track, back down the hill, panting, back to the house.

The car was parked outside. I knocked and tried turning the handle. It didn't open. I looked in at the window. The gowk was there at the table, eating, reading a newspaper. Mum was nowhere to be seen.

I tapped on the glass.

He didn't react.

I tapped again.

He looked up and gestured to the front door.

I went back and stood, waiting for him to open it, jiggling from foot to foot. Rain dripped off my hair and down my face.

'Where's Mum?'

He pointed at my shoes.

I kicked them off and went on through. 'Where's Mum?' I asked again.

'They've taken her to hospital; she's having tests.' He went back to his plate. He scraped the last scraps of food from it, pushed it aside, and carried on reading.

Hospital? I stood as still as stone. 'When will she be home?'

'Tomorrow. Maybe.'

It was odd. He wasn't saying a thing about the water dripping from me on to his floor. Tears pricked the inside of my eyelids. I blinked them away fast. 'I'm hungry.'

I waited. Well, if he wasn't going to give me anything to eat, I'd have to find it myself.

I went to the bread bin and lifted the lid. I glanced back at him, not knowing if he'd try to stop me. He didn't stir.

I took out a loaf of bread, cut off a slice, smeared it with butter, found a bit of cold chicken in the fridge and made myself a thick sandwich. I put it on a plate and took myself and the plate to the bottom stair.

'Come and sit at the table,' he said, his head still down in the paper. I took myself and my plate to the furthest corner of the table from him, pulled out a stool and sat down. When I was finished, I took the plate to the sink and washed it under a trickle from the tap, trying not to make any noise. I dried it and opened the cupboard to put it back. It slipped from my hand and fell.

I froze. But it didn't break.

I replaced the plate and closed the cupboard door and looked under my eyelashes at him. He was being really strange. His shoulders were stiff. His Adam's apple slid up and down in his throat but he didn't say a word. He had the paper open but he was frowning and he didn't turn a page.

I went to the stairs; he didn't call me back. I went upstairs to my room, avoiding the two creaky bits halfway, and closed my door behind me and let out my breath: *whoo*. I took off my wet clothes and dumped them on the floor. Tomorrow, he'd said. Mum would be back tomorrow.

He'd sounded peculiar. And the way he'd been staring at his paper was as if he was frightened of something. I shivered. I'd smelled fear down the steps in the cellar, too. Fear and sweat and rotting food. And I'd seen a face; at least, I thought I had, something round and pale looking up at me from the bottom of the steps.

I crept into bed, hauled Woody out from under the pillow where I kept him safe, opened the window wide and stared out, holding him close. Wind lifted my hair while rain blew in on us.

Twenty-four

In the morning there was no call from Mum to get up.

No call came at all. When I went down for breakfast, he was putting on his shoes. 'Oh, you.' He looked distracted. 'Hurry up. I'm not having you here in the house when I'm gone.'

'Will Mum…' I stopped. 'Will Mum be here when I get back from school?'

'I shall go to the hospital as soon as it's visiting time and see how she is.'

I swallowed. 'Can I come, too?'

'No. It's too far to come back for you; I really haven't got the time. Come on, get ready. I expect your mother will be out in a couple of days.'

'You said "today" yesterday.'

'I said "maybe".'

'Don't you know?'

'No, I don't. And please don't shout.'

'Is she…' I stopped. If I asked if she was pregnant, that might make it true. I swallowed hard, but could feel my face going red.

'Now don't cry, Percival. I've enough to cope with as it is. I shall probably have an early night tonight so make sure you're back on time.'

'I'll fetch myself some bread.'

'There's no time for that,' he snapped. 'You should have got up at the proper time if you wanted breakfast. Breakfast at seven forty-five. Put on your shoes, hurry.'

'Kyle! Feet down. Lovely knees, but I don't want to see them at table. Percy, your health-survey form, please.'

I flushed.

'Have you forgotten it again? Hmm. Then would you go to the office in break and get another? Ask your mother after school to fill it in, right?'

'I can't, she won't be there,' I mumbled.

Mr Magnus was shifting through papers on his desk and didn't hear me. No one did.

'Or ask Mr Bockley,' he went on.

No way. Perhaps I could fill it in myself. If I wrote in block capitals, it could look all right.

'Do you want all of that?' It was break and Mary Ann was peeling a banana and taking a bite.

She stopped in mid-chew. 'Why, do you want some?'

'I had no breakfast.' I flushed, embarrassed.

'Didn't they give you any?'

'She's in hospital.'

'Oh.'

'He says she's having tests.'

'What about him? Didn't he give you anything to eat?'

I shook my head. 'I don't think he's going to.'

'Of course he will! You can always come to ours if he doesn't. Here.' She handed me the banana. I gulped it down in two.

Then at lunch I ate corn on the cob and cottage pie and a slice of apple pie and put an apple in my pocket for later, in case.

'Right. You arrive at Watford at 10:42. How long do you have to wait for the next train to Exeter?' It was sums from railway timetables again. We all groaned.

'Percy, why aren't you getting on with your work? What number are you on?' Mr Magnus was leaning over the table.

'Six.'

'Only six? Goodness, you're way behind. So, how long must you wait?'

I stared down at the book.

Mary Ann nudged me. 'Forty minutes.'

'Are you telling Percy the answers? He'll have no idea if you tell him. Come on, Percy, you're easily capable. Move on to the next one. At what time does the 12:21 from Crewe reach Yeovil, and where would you change and how long would you have to wait when you change?' He moved away. 'Kyle, yes, arrival and departure times at a single station are about the same, unless you're changing trains.'

'Not when you're in Bentham,' Tim called out. 'The train's sat there for five minutes.'

'Well, you try improving the timetable then! Now shhh, not so loud.'

Mary Ann slid her arithmetic book closer. 'It'll be all right, you know. Look at me - I was in hospital and I came out again.'

'You weren't pregnant.'

'Oh wow, is she going to have a baby?'

'I don't know! There's something wrong.'

'Having a baby isn't wrong.'

'Mary Ann.' Mr Magnus was back. 'Which number have you reached?'

Quickly she slid back her book.

'Let's see. Twelve. Not bad.'

'I don't understand this one,' she said, 'about the train getting to Andover. I don't think it stops there at all, so do I just put that?'

'Doesn't stop at Andover!' Mr Magnus stood back in pretend horror. 'Daniel, can you spring to her aid?'

'Two hours thirty-two minutes.' Louise jumped in instead.

'Thank you, Louise, but I was asking Daniel. Well?'

'No, it's two hours twelve minutes.'

'Correct. Now, Percy.' He tapped me lightly on the head. 'Any you don't do now, you'll have to finish again for homework, as well as getting on with the story we started the other day.'

'She'll be there when you get back,' Mary Ann whispered.

'Mmm.' I crossed my fingers behind my back, hoping she was right.

'Friday's going to take off like a rocket.' Mr Magnus was striding among our tables. 'We're going to visit Victorian Seggleswick. I want you on your best behaviour. Think: the impression you make matters and counts.'

'Can we dress up in costume, like?'

'That would be fun, Zoe, wouldn't it. Your skirt and shirt and blue sweatshirts aren't very nineteenth-century, are they? Why is that?'

He waited. 'Don't all shout out at once! Percy, yes: you're the only one with a hand up.'

'Because Zoe'd be in a woollen frock with black wool

stockings and a white pinafore over them, and she'd have lace-up boots with wooden soles on her feet. Clogs, like.'

'Genius, Percy. I can tell you've been reading up on the subject. You're full of surprises. But no, you'll all be in your usual school uniform. I want you to write a description of your home, as it is today. Next week, after our Victorian expedition, I'll be asking you to describe it as it was then.'

'Please, Mr Magnus.'

'Yes, Tim?'

'Our house is new. So how can I describe it in the past?'

'How indeed. Think about it.'

Tim put down his hand, puzzled.

'We're fortunate enough to be having a historian with us on that day, Dr Elizabeth Gabriel. She will no doubt fill in the gaps in my knowledge. For now, pens to paper, please. Write the first sentence about your home and its immediate surroundings.'

I turned to a fresh page in my book, happy to be going into the past. I wouldn't write about the gowk's house. I closed my eyes, picturing the bank on the corner of the market square. It shimmered and dissolved, and in its place was a two-storey shop and house. The door was open and I could see leather saddles and boots and strips of leather hanging from the walls and beams in the ceiling. Two men were at the door and they were looking towards the market cross where people were gathering.

'P.' I was being kicked. 'P! He's coming, start writing.'

I opened my eyes. Daniel's face swam into focus. I straightened my back and shook my head free.

'Right, books away, finish it next time,' Mr Magnus called at the buzz of the bell.

The buzzing reverberated in my head and turned to a clanging.

'Stand!'

We stood.

'Line up!'

We lined up.

'File out. Girls first! I said, girls first!' The master whacked a boy who'd got out of line. 'In silence!'

But by then the news had reached all of us, whispered from the front back down the rows when the master wasn't looking. 'The stocks! Man in stocks!'

We left the schoolroom and burst from the doors in a knot and tore past the barrel organ in our haste to get to the market place.

'The Shambles!' I peeled off with my friends and ran first to where they butchered meat. 'There!'

Seeing me coming, a butcher pointed with a bloodied cleaver to a bucket. 'You can take that. Bring it back when you're done!' he shouted after us as we grabbed it and ran.

We pushed our way to the front of the small crowd in front of the market cross. A soft, mouldy orange shot from the hand of a woman. 'Take that for your curses!' There was a squelchy thud as it hit its mark, right on the chin of the man in the stocks. It was Morphet's father. He was on a wooden bench, his legs stretched out through the holes in front of him, held in place by the bottom plank. He couldn't wipe away the fleshy sticky mess that trickled down his chin and on to his jacket because his arms were imprisoned in two other holes in the upper plank.

'Why're you in there, Amos Bibber? What've you done this time, Amos Bibber?' we called out.

He looked shifty. 'It's nowt to do with you.' His head drooped.

A man came from the town hall with a placard that he hung round the prisoner's neck.

AMOS BIBBER, DRUNK AND ABUSIVE

Then he took an egg from a box in front of the stocks and threw it. It missed. But it broke on the top plank, right beside the prisoner, so close that he turned his head aside. It was an old egg, see, and stank of all the gases of Hell. Yellow yolk dribbled down the wood and we cheered. Passers-by stopped, some to jeer, some to shake their heads in sorrow; a few ignored him.

I plunged my hand into the butcher's bucket and pulled out slippery red stuff and threw it. It spattered on his cheeks and nose, and we cheered again, me and my friends. It dribbled down over his mouth. He shook his head, trying to stop it going in, and failing. He tried to spit it back at us and we laughed. 'You can't get us! You can't get us!'

'Pass over that bucket, Benjamin. Give us some!' My friends got stuck in.

'Bibber by name, bibber by nature!' cried out a woman. 'Sign the Pledge before it's too late. "Wine is a mocker, strong drink is raging" as the Good Book says.'

'You hark that, Welly Cox?' screeched Ma Cox as Welly skulked away. 'You trial and burden, you nothingforgoodsome.'

'Sign the Pledge, sign the Pledge!' we cried gleefully, pelting Morphet's father with more slimy offal.

I was just straightening from taking another handful of offal from the bucket when I caught sight of Morphet, hanging back on the corner, snivelling. As I looked, he wiped his nose on his sleeve, but the tears still came, I could see from where I was. I pushed my way over. 'Here,' I offered him some slippery red gunk.

He shook his head.

'Go on! Throw it at him. Get your own back.'

'No-o-o.' His eyes were red. Snot ran down his face. 'You're to stop it. Please stop. I won't half catch it when they let him go. The more you hit him, the more he'll beat me afterwards,' he sobbed. He half charged at me, and ran off.

The stuff was still in my hand and I wanted to throw it but wasn't sure now if I should. I dithered.

'Throw it, P!'

I stared at the ball in my hand. How had it got there? I threw it hard at Harry, hoisted my bag on my shoulder and fled, through the school gates, down towards the river and the graveyard, alone, leaving them, mouths agape.

Twenty-five

At the lych-gate two familiar figures were waiting: Mother, with Grace at her side. 'We thought we should find you here,' said Mother, one hand resting on her tummy. 'We were taking swill to our pig, but I'm heavy and ill at ease today, so Grace will take me home. Would you feed Mollie instead, Benjamin?'

I took the pail of pigswill from Grace and walked on up to the common pastureland. There were nine pigs in there, but only one was brown with white spots, our Mollie. She was the fattest, too. In a few weeks' time when the days shortened, Father and I would be driving her down to the market place, to the Shambles, to be slaughtered, so we'd have meat all through the winter.

Most of the pigs were rooting about in the undergrowth. Mollie, lazy as ever, was lying under a tree, snoring. When I climbed over the gate and clicked my tongue, she didn't stir. I picked up a stone and banged the side of the pail: 'Mollie! Mollie!' That got her moving all right. She hefted herself to her feet and plodded over, ears flopping forward in her eagerness to thrust her snout in the bucket to get at the peelings and eggshells. It was all I could do to hold it steady and stop her knocking it over. As it was, she managed to scatter a fair few of the peelings on the ground. She rasped them up with her tongue, along with ounces of dust from the churned-up earth. She shoved her head back in the pail and shook it hard, making me let go; I was no match for her, she was way heavier.

I climbed back on to the five-bar gate, just getting my leg out of the way in time as Mollie rubbed her massive bulk against the wood to have a good scratch. I leaned over to help, digging my fingers into her back. The hairs were rough and dusty under my nails, the flesh solid. Dust rose up in puffs as I scratched, and she groaned her pleasure. I scratched and scratched and scratched, losing myself in the movement.

'Hello there. Admiring the pigs, I see.'

I almost fell off the gate. My fingers were still scratching a brown pig, and it was still grunting away but the woman at my side was in jeans and a thick jumper. I recognised her, too, even though she was wearing glasses this time.

'A fine couple of pigs, aren't they?' She glanced shrewdly at me and chattered on as if I wasn't flustered; she didn't know why I was, of course. I was whirling from one 'me' to another; the changes now were all so sudden. There wasn't even any pail at my feet where I - where Benjamin - had let it fall. Nor were there so many pigs. Just the one. And one other, I saw: a black one poked its nose out of a straw-bale shelter and grunted its way across to us, shoving the brown one aside.

'I'm Liz,' she said, 'hello.' She scratched the black pig between its ears.

'Hello,' I mumbled, my head well down. I didn't want her remembering me; it had been her cellar.

'What's your name?'

'Ben.' I couldn't help it; that's how it came out.

'I've seen you before, haven't I?'

Just then I heard a car. I saw a familiar flash of silver, and I was glad. I was off the gate and running. 'Got to go.' Mum might be in the car. I didn't care if the woman thought I was rude or unfriendly.

As I ran down the path to the house, the door was shutting. I pressed the bell: *dee dee dee dah dah.*

The door opened. 'Oh. Hello. You'd better come in.' But he didn't move from the doorway until I was almost nose to shoulder with him; he seemed in a sort of daze.

'Mum?' I asked, looking beyond him.

He shook his head. 'She's not here.'

'How is she?' I shrugged off my bag and knelt to take off my shoes.

'Don't leave that bag lying there,' he muttered before I'd even got the second shoe off.

I glared at his retreating back, picked up the bag, took it up to my room, dumped it on my bed and ran back downstairs.

'How's Mum?' I asked again.

'Don't shout; I can hear you fine. She's all right,' he answered, his head in the fridge. 'One test went a bit wrong, so they're keeping her in a while longer.'

'How much longer?'

'I said, a while. Now stop pestering me, will you? It's bad enough not having her at home,' he said in a low voice.

'Is she all right?'

He turned away from me. For a moment I thought he was going to cry. I stayed rooted to the spot, watching him, frightened. I'd never seen him like this before.

'Go to your room!' he hissed, turning and seeing me

standing there.

I sat on my bed, worrying. What if he wasn't letting me see her because he was hiding something from me? What if Mum wasn't pregnant but was sick, really sick? What if Mum never came back? I picked up Woody and set him on the windowsill and leaned on it myself and stared out. I wished Mum was here. If only I could see her. What if…. I stopped that thought in its tracks, I wouldn't let it come. But it rushed back just the same. Was Mum ill because I'd cursed him, the cuckoo, the gowk, and the curse had landed in the wrong place, on her? Or on me? I went all jittery at the thought. I didn't know what to do.

My stomach rumbled. If Mum was here she'd have cake or sandwiches to eat and we'd laugh together – so long as he wasn't around, I thought glumly. It felt awful to be hungry, but he'd sent me upstairs, so it didn't look as if he was going to cook or anything. I'd picked some more blackberries for Mum the other day and had hidden them right at the back of the fridge and never given them to her.

I sat up straight. I'd go down and eat those, and see if there was any chicken left.

I tiptoed downstairs. He was in the armchair right in the corner, eating something on toast, staring into space, not reading his paper or anything.

I took out the bowl and, keeping my back to him, shoved my fingers into the berries and scooped them into my mouth.

'You silly boy. What is it with you and blackberries?' He'd come up. 'Don't you know that the Devil's spat on them?'

I stared at my hand. 'The Devil spat on these?'

'From September onwards.'

A red-horned creature with a forked tail spitting on my blackberries? I grinned at him. 'You're wrong. It's from November. They're fine.' I scooped up more.

'Well, I don't want you eating them. All myths have a basis in fact. Oh, for Pete's sake, here, have the rest of my toast.'

He passed it to me. It had a thick layer of toasted cheese. I stared at it, at his toothmarks in the cheese. I loved toasted cheese.

But I shook my head. I didn't want to eat what he'd been eating.

'I'm not much of a father to you, am I,' he said gruffly.

I was surprised. He sounded sorry, a bit. He was holding out an arm stiffly.

I ignored it. He sighed. 'Please yourself. I'm not making you anything else. It's this or nothing. Eat, and then go back to your room.'

He waited beside me as I ate.

Twenty-six

It was too early for bed, so I started writing about the house, not this one, but the other one. I put paper on the windowsill and started.

'Before it was a bank, the house was…'

…and I heard a voice call: 'Six o'clock o' the morning and God's in His heaven.' It was the knocker-up across the way, banging on a door with his stick. I opened the bedroom window and leaned out from my bed and watched him. I still had some time to lie abed, a bit of time before the milkman would be along with his pail and Mother and Father would be telling us to rise. Below, a group of girls flitted by in the darkness, swathed in shawls, clogs clattering, as they passed on their way from the lodging house to the mill. A farmer's cart came rattling down the hill, the calves in the back struggling to stay on their feet with each jerk and lurch of the cart. The noises were all as usual.

But another noise than these had woken me. I went out on to the dark landing. The door to Mother and Father's room opened and Father stood in the opening.

'Benjamin, run and fetch Mrs Spencer. Your mother's time has come.'

When I got back with Mrs Spencer, Father was in the shop with a candle, smoking. He knocked his pipe out on the windowsill and took her upstairs, then came back down. Grace and Jane and John were all up and dressed and in the kitchen. 'You be mother,' he said to Grace. 'Make the porridge and the tea. You lot,' to us, 'to the table.'

Grace fetched the can of milk from the pantry and ladled it out into the pan of porridge that had been warming all night. She stirred it till it was ready then doled it out so we each had a bowlful which we stiffened with salt, the Scottish way as Father had taught us. He barely touched his.

'Get out in the air,' he told us when we were done, 'stay away as long as you can, I don't want you here under my feet. You, Benjamin, look after the others. Off you go, off!'

So we did. We went to the pigs and watched them and scratched them. We went to the field and talked to the cows and when they came right up to us at the gate, we blew down their wide nostrils and they huffed back at us spreading puffs of grass-cow smell over us, staring from their large, liquid brown eyes. One daringly stuck out a thick tongue and licked Jane who managed not to squeal and move away. We went to the apple tree with its branches hanging over the road and scrumped apples from them, and ate them. But our hearts weren't in any of it. We wanted to be home. I needed to be home.

I woke up when it wasn't properly light, my heart racing. At first, I couldn't work out where I was. Then my surroundings took shape. I was at the window, still dressed in school trousers and blue school sweatshirt. But I should be home! I scrunched up my shoulders and shook my head and looked out of the modern white-framed window. What home?

I splashed water on my face and scrubbed it dry and brushed my teeth. I even combed my hair. Then I sat on the bed watching the clock at my bedside.

7:44.

I got off the bed and went downstairs.

'You're late, young man,' was his greeting as I went to the bread bin and took out a loaf.

I whirled round, bread knife in my hand. 'It's a quarter to eight.'

'Breakfast is at half past seven. And put that knife down.'

'You said 7:45.'

'Did I? When was that?'

'Yesterday.'

'You must have misheard me. Please, hurry up. Shoes on, jacket on, it's drizzling out there.'

'You haven't given me my dinner money.' We were outside. He locked the door and pocketed the bunch of keys.

'That's for your mother to do.'

'So can I see her? Will you take me this afternoon?'

'It isn't convenient. I told you. Write her a card and I'll take it to her.'

'I haven't got a card and I can't fetch one now you've gone and locked us out!' I exploded.

'You're off the map, you're so cheeky!'

'That's stupid. Seggleswick's right in the middle of the British Isles!'

'That's enough! And don't look at me like that. Percival, I've no energy for this.'

I felt sick. There was something seriously wrong with Mum. I knew it. His face was as drained of colour as his grey jacket, as if he'd had no sleep, no air.

'I sincerely trust that you are not so impudent in class,' he muttered, half at me. 'Make sure you're back in good time after school,' and with that parting shot he strode off down the path. A bank of mist came rolling in. Through it I could just see him get in the car and drive off, vanishing in the cloud.

There I was, washed, dressed, school bag at my feet, too early for school, and hungry.

The mist grew thicker. It hung round me like a million ghosts. I could see nothing beyond my own footsteps and a small circle around them. Ten steps. I counted. Ducks huddled on the green weed in the shallows of the beck and never raised their heads as I went past. No house could be seen, only the stone walls at my side with their scraggy shawls of moss and lichen. A pinprick shower of moisture clung to me as I moved.

On the slab bridge over the beck I almost tripped. I reached out for the old iron railing. It was as cold and clammy as dead men's fingers. I shook my hands free. I got down on hands and knees and hauled up a clutch of watercress from the side of the beck. Mum didn't like picking it here, but I didn't care. She wasn't here, was she. Besides, chewing anything, even sharp peppery cress, was better than nothing.

I heard the rumble of wheels, and got to my feet as a cart trundled by with something lying in it, on straw, something large that wasn't a cow. A passer-by took off his cap. I followed the cart to the Hearse House opposite the church. Its doors were open, and a man waited there, bareheaded. 'Take tha' cap off, lad; the dead deserve respect even if it is Welly Cox,' he said sharply, but I was already doing that. He and the driver lifted a corpse from the straw on to a bier and the doors shut again. 'The ninth death in so many days,' he muttered. Then, seeing me still standing there, 'Get away, go home, Benjamin.'

And then I was back in my skin today, as if nothing had happened.

Mum told me once that dreams only take a few seconds, maybe a minute or two but not much more, no matter how long they seem when you're dreaming them. That was what it was like.

I walked on, slapping my shoes down hard on the tarmac, making sure that it was tarmac and not dried mud and grit. This was where I was, this was my life. Or was it the other? I wouldn't mind living in the other life. I had family there, Mother, Father, brother and sisters, and friends, too. I belonged. What had I here? I gnawed my finger. It was still too early for school. I'd go into town to hang about. I felt coiled like a spring, pent up like a caged lion.

By the market square there was a gap between two buildings that I hadn't noticed before, a gap just wide enough for a man. I stepped into it. The paving was crumbling and uneven, and spattered white with bird droppings, and from the smell you could tell people had used the ginnel to piss in. High above me the roofs of the old buildings on either side leaned towards each other, letting through only a glimmer of light. I passed a walled-up door, and another, and saw ahead of me a blank wall. Dead end. I was about to retrace my steps when I heard the sound of scuffles ahead and a cry, 'Let me g-go!' It broke off. It was Morphet!

I ran straight at the blank wall. It wasn't a dead end at all.

'Leave me alone!' Nor was it Morphet. It was another voice I knew.

The wall took a sudden sharp turn left, zig-zagged past a door and came out into a courtyard. And in the courtyard was Harry. He couldn't shout now because two big youths had him by the arms and one was pinching his nose; the third had his mouth forced open and was pouring clear liquid from a bottle down his throat. 'You wanted to taste it, so, here y'are, taste!' There was a girl there, too, laughing and taking photographs. At least, I think that's what she was doing but I didn't stop to look. I launched myself out of that alley like a jack-in-the-box, screaming, 'Stop that! Stop!', and I knocked the bottle out of the youth's hand and kicked the legs of one of those holding him. The bottle-pourer came for me and I butted his stomach with all my might. He bent over double. One down, two to go, but then I was knocked to the ground and was being kicked. There was a ringing in my ears but I didn't care, my blood was up, and I was back on my feet.

'You'd have me, would you, you pissbag!' shouted the bottle-pourer. He tripped me and I fell again. As I fell, I saw Harry struggling to get to me but one of the big lads was holding him off.

'No! Run, Harry!'

He understood, and broke free and ran. Divide the bullies and we'd have more chance. After a moment's hesitation, one of the lads followed him, but I didn't think he'd catch Harry. Another youth sloped off.

That left the bottle-pourer. 'Get up.' He stood over me.

I got groggily to my feet.

His hand flashed out and he slapped me. I rocked on my feet

but didn't fall, not this time. 'Go on, flit, you cheeky beggar. Back down Spooky Alley where you came from.' He shoved me towards the alley.

I went, my tummy lurching. There was no need to stay.

The hairs on the back of my neck stood up as I heard the whisper of clothing behind me.

'Good lad.' The words blew into my ear.

I stopped, my heart thudding.

No one was in the dark ginnel but me.

When I came out on to the market square, a car drove past, and another. A woman came out of the newsagent's with a ping of the door. Other shop doors were opening, there were people around. And Louise was passing. 'Pooh.' She pinched her nose. 'What've you been doing? It stinks down there. And look at you. Have you been *fighting*, P? You're a right mess.'

'Huh.' I was too drained to answer. My head was throbbing and my side was sore and I could taste blood from my face.

'Are you coming to school like *that*?' You should have heard the scorn in her voice!

She was right; I'd be in trouble. If Mum was there she'd clean me up. That was when I remembered the stone water troughs and the spring, up the steep track. I went up a roughly tarmacked road and found them there, in exactly the same place, even if the water was murkier. I squatted down so as to splash away the blood with water. I ran wet fingers through my hair and scrubbed away the dirt on my sleeve. I had to see Mum, had to make sure she'd come back from hospital. Something awful might happen if I didn't.

Twenty-seven

We'd stayed away with the pigs and cows and such as long as we could, Grace and John and Jane and I. When we got back, Mother was still upstairs with Mrs Spencer and Aunt had arrived from Pipton and was upstairs, too. Father was in the shop with a customer. 'It will take time,' he had said to us. 'I'd as soon work as worry.' Grace went into the kitchen, taking John and Jane with her, to bake bread, and I stayed behind.

'I should be greatly obliged if you would untie the reins for me, lad, so that I may be on my way.' The customer's horse pawed the ground, wanting to be off.

I freed the leather reins looped through the iron ring in the wall and untied the horse. There was a commotion further along, and I stretched to see. The constable was hurrying down the road, holding Morphet by one ear, twisted awkwardly and limping.

'Young rascal; there goes a criminal in the making!' The customer clicked his tongue at the horse and wheeled it round to get going.

'What's he done, sir?'

But he wasn't listening. I glanced behind at the saddlery then ran after the constable. I wasn't the only one. Passers-by were gathering. 'What's he done?' I asked again.

'He was caught red-handed stealing turnips, he and another lad. T'other one got away.'

'He'll be for it now!' Ma Cox was there, small eyes gleaming to see another in trouble for a change.

The constable marched Morphet through the small crowd and on up the steps to the town hall. The frosted-glass door swung shut behind them.

'Where's he taking him?' I tugged at Obadiah Baynes' sleeve. He'd come out of his drinks' shop to see what the commotion was.

'To see the magistrate, I'll be bound.'

'It's no more and no less than he deserves, helping himself to food others have planted.'

'Isn't it Amos Bibber's son? There's bad blood there. Flow where it will, bad blood will out!'

The comments were falling around Morphet like hail.

'He's hungry!' I turned fiercely to them, and with that, I was up the steps and hammering at the door. But they wouldn't let me in. A woman standing just inside pointed upwards. 'Top floor.' I took the stairs two at a time, not pausing to think. I wriggled my way into the courthouse. There was Morphet, standing small and alone before the magistrate, his hands behind his back, gripped so tightly I could see the white of his knuckles.

'Is the boy's father here? I have asked for him,' said the magistrate. 'Is he here?'

'He'll be at Obadiah's,' said the constable, 'sozzled, as usual. It's even worse since Welly died.'

There was a rumble of agreement.

'Send the boy to the gaol.'

'Whip him!'

'Put him on a ship and send him to Australia.'

'Or the workhouse and have them punish him!'

'Workhouse? Too good for him. He's set on a downward path already; he'd be nobbut a drain on the town's resources there.' That was Ma Cox, who had followed me up the stairs, shriller even than the others.

'Silence! I will not have this noise in court.' The magistrate banged his gavel on the desk.

I put up my hand. 'Please, sir.'

He peered down at me. Encouraged, I spoke up. 'Don't punish him. It's not right! He's hungry. He's always hungry.'

'This is most irregular. Who are you, boy?'

'Benjamin Waugh, sir.'

'The saddler's lad.'

'Thank you, constable. We can see that he's not shy at speaking for himself.'

Morphet was eyeing me hopefully.

'You see, sir, his father won't feed him, and all he earns from working for the tannery goes to his father and he spends it all on drink. It isn't right!' I repeated, 'Sir.'

The magistrate stared at Morphet, and then at me, and then at Morphet again. From a tin he took a pinch of snuff. He laid it on the back of his hand then sniffed it up his nostrils and let out a sneeze as loud as any donkey's.

'Here's a fine champion!' he said finally. 'Well, how do you say we let Morphet off this time, and you, Benjamin, make sure that he gets a square meal? And keep an eye on him. Because next time,' he pointed the gavel at me, 'it will be gaol.

Understood?'

'Yes, sir. Thank you, sir.'

'Release the prisoner into this lad's care.' Bang went the gavel.

I held out a hand to Morphet and he took it and we beat a hasty retreat before the magistrate changed his mind. I took him home, not through the shop but round the back. The kitchen door was open and the smell of warm bread stronger than the rawer smells of leather and horse that hung around our corner of the market square. I grabbed a loaf before Grace could stop me. 'Here.' I stuck my fingers into the hot bread and tore it in two and gave half to Morphet who sank his teeth into it at once, he was that hungry.

'Benjamin?' I looked up, surprised to hear the flutey voice. It was Aunt Patience from Pipton. 'Is that you?' She came to the door. 'Who is this? What do you think you are doing?'

Morphet stared at her, cheeks bulging with bread. Like a frightened deer he fled, clutching the half-loaf to him.

'You don't have to… go,' I finished. Too late; he was out of sight. 'He's Morphet,' I told Aunt.

'And who's Morphet when he's at home? Oh, never mind that now. Come indoors, lad, I haven't time for discussion. But you should have asked first.' She took the steaming kettle off the hob. 'I'm back up now to your mother. Go and find Grace and the others.'

Twenty-eight

'Percy, you're late.'

Was it any wonder? How could I not be late with so much happening in my Benjamin life? I slid into my seat. Harry was already there at the table, whispering to Daniel. They were looking over at me.

'Your health-survey form, please,' Mr Magnus held out his hand for it. 'Still not signed? Tomorrow, all right, young man? Let's hope that you've got your historical wits about you instead. It's Victorian Seggleswick this morning.' He addressed the whole class now. 'We'll be setting off in a moment.' He glanced at his watch, and then at the woman who appeared in the door opening. 'Ah, there you are. Welcome. Boys and girls, this is Dr Elizabeth Gabriel who's joining us today - , archeologist, historian and biographer. Kyle, spell archeologist for us, please.'

'A-r-k-i-o-l-o-g-i-s-t.'

'Percy, can you help him?'

'Er...' Daniel was giving me a thumbs-up.

'Daniel?'

Daniel spelt it out as I looked at the woman who'd come in, in her deep red skirt and boots and yellow jumper. It was Liz.

'Jackets on, and line up in twos outside.' Tim was with Harry, Daniel with Mary Ann. I was on my own, but right behind them. Daniel turned. 'Wow, P. Fighting for Harry.'

Off we set. Liz smiled as I passed her. 'We meet again.'

'Oh?' I heard Mr Magnus ask.

'I've seen Ben around a few times,' she said quietly.

'Percy.'

'What?'

'His name's Percy.'

'Oh, I'm sure he said Ben yesterday, at the pigs. Trust me, I always was hopeless at names.' From the way she looked at me, I don't think she meant that, and there was laughter in her voice as they moved on.

'Gather round.' Mr Magnus called us to a halt. 'Daniel? How can you listen if you're talking to Mary Ann? Thank you. Now then, this alley we're walking through used to be a main thoroughfare. In those days there would have been traffic and plenty of it. Not cars and lorries, of course, but horse-drawn. It's called Kirkgate. Can anyone tell me why?'

'It leads to the church,' I said. Mary Ann grinned.

'It does: kirk, church. What else can anyone think to tell me about it? Look around you, look above the doors, see if you can see anything written there.'

'The Spencers lived in this house,' I said, pointing to a charcoal-grey door. 'You know, the ones with the big gravestone in the churchyard, the ones who all died?' Everyone died, I knew that, and people got sick. But not Mum, please not Mum.

Mr Magnus looked at me with interest. So did Liz. 'Did they? How do you know they lived there?'

'Hey - Spencer, like Mary Ann?' Daniel asked, nudging her.

I shrugged. I'd said enough already.

But I couldn't keep my mouth shut. As we moved on, Mr Magnus described which shop had been where, how the streets had been lit by vegetable gas and how vile that had smelled and I'd had to chime in to tell them about other smells like dog turds and how you collected them by the bucketful, didn't I, and about the smell of horses and cows and geese and all, and the butchers in the Shambles. After that I tried to go round with the class as if I'd never been here before in the past.

'Of course, even on a muggy autumn day like this,' he said, looking up at the gathering clouds, 'you'd be dressed in - mm? What would you be dressed in?'

'Wool,' answered Zoe. So she had been listening the other morning.

'It felt really itchy,' I told her.

'Itchy? Did it?' Liz, Dr Gabriel, had heard me.

'Yeh.' I shut up then for the rest of the morning.

It was almost dinner-time when we got back to school.

'I've forgotten my dinner money,' I told Mr Magnus.

'You're forgetting everything, aren't you. Are you all right, young Percy? You do seem strange. Forgetting forms and money, and then talking the way you do about Seggleswick.'

'And he saved Harry,' chimed in Daniel.

'Did he indeed. Open your books at page fifty-three, everyone, and get on with the exercise there; we've a bit of time before the dinner bell goes.' He came over to our table. 'What's up?' he asked quietly.

'I think Mum's dying,' I blurted out.

He eyed me, startled. 'Is she? And is she at home?'

'She's in hospital. He won't take me.'

'He? Oh, I suppose you mean Mr Bockley.'

I gave a nod.

'Where is he?'

'At work, I s'pose.'

He rested a hand on my shoulder. 'All right. I'll ring him. Now, class,' he raised his voice, 'who can furnish me with the answers to the first lot of questions. Yes, Kyle?'

'I thought you said she was having tests.' Mary Ann shuffled her chair closer. 'Why do you say she's dying?'

I clenched and unclenched my fingers. How could I explain about the feeling I had deep inside, the sinking feeling, the knowing that someone precious was about to leave me.

When she saw that I wasn't answering, she shut up. Harry, didn't say anything either. Louise kept peering at me over her glasses.

'Line up quietly,' said Mr Magnus as the bell went. He said I could go and eat even though I'd forgotten my dinner money. Daniel and Tim and Harry and Mary Ann and even Louise sat with me and I had cheese and bacon macaroni with carrots, and pear and date fudge pudding, but when I finished it all, it lay like a stone in my stomach.

Mr Magnus called me into a quiet room. 'Now then. I've spoken to your stepfather.'

'He's not my stepfather!'

'All right, calm down. Now listen. What he told me was that they have to do various tests because they don't know what's the matter. I gather that she reacted badly to one test and they're keeping her under observation.'

'Is it because she's going to have a baby? Or are the tests for cancer?'

'Hold on.' He looked gravely at me. 'I didn't ask for specifics.'

'So is she going to die?'

'Why, Percy? Even if – and it's a big if – your mother had cancer, say, they'll have caught it in time and they'll treat her for it.'

I wanted to believe him. But the feeling inside wasn't fading. I had to see her.

'Now, back to class with you.'

After class, Harry and Daniel asked if I'd like to play football and it wasn't Cherry Arse this time, it was five-aside football with them and Tim and others. I stayed and played and no one teased me, not for my name, not for anything. We only stopped as the clouds became dark and dense and threatening.

It began to drizzle but I walked only slowly back to the house. That way it was more likely that Mum would be back when I got there. If I walked quickly, I knew she wouldn't be.

She wasn't. Nor was the car. I can't have walked slowly enough. I kicked the doorstep. I didn't know what to do with myself, I felt so restless.

A cat walked back along the beck with me, keeping close to me as if for shelter, the bell round its neck tinkling. I looked down at it, remembering another cat, just as black as this one, and with a bell round its neck too. 'Polly,' I whispered. It miaowed at me, but came no further than the slab bridge.

I went into the churchyard and picked a rose from a bush near the gate. I had to tug quite hard to break it off, and then a thorn went and jabbed my thumb and I had to pinch it out and suck away the blood. Then I wandered round the churchyard carrying the rose till I reached the Spencers and sat down there on the grass that covered the grave. It was strange to think of Mary Ann and her family lying there below, but not scary. I'd never felt scared here. The sun had gone in again, and I hoisted up the collar of my jacket against the drizzle, and leaned back against the tombstone and closed my eyes as the clock tolled the hour.

The tolling grew louder. One - two -... I opened my eyes to a huge church tower looming over me against a night sky, looking as if it would come crashing down at any moment. Three - four - tolled the clock. There were dark smells around: stale sweat, soot and horse manure, and the creak and clatter of carts and horses' hooves on cobbles, and shouting. I was sitting on a huge slab, one of many that stretched like enormous paving stones, laid end to end, all the way to a low wall beyond; the moonlight showed up the skull and crossbones engraved on it. On the slabs were the raggedy shapes of boys and girls, some huddled together, others alone, their arms and legs like matchsticks, so thin they could snap; you could see the bones move beneath their rags. On the other side of the low wall it was all light and bustle and noise, but here it was quiet, and no one crossed the wall to come to us.

In my dream I saw the face of the boy closest to me, and it was Morphet's. He was dressed in rags and his feet were bare, black with dirt and hard as leather, with cracks running deep into his heels. I put out a hand to him. He struggled to take it but the slabs between us widened and kept us from touching. I stretched my hand out further and saw that my hand was a grown-up's, and no matter how far I stretched my arm, my hand still couldn't reach Morphet.

That's when I woke up and found myself in pouring rain, still on the Spencer grave, with an uneasy sensation in my head. I put up my hands and squeezed, to get rid of the tightness there. As I did so, there came a muffled sound of voices and the tinkle of tea cups, as if on the other side of a door. My eyes blurred.

I pushed on a door to open it.

Twenty-nine

'There you are, young sir.' An arm snaked round my shoulders and drew me into the parlour. As on John's birthday all the candles were lit from the sconces on the wall and on the mantelpiece and the tall oak dresser. And yet this time it cannot have been anyone's birthday. The table was laden with food and chairs, and people filled the room. They were all in black. I looked down, and saw that I was too, in black trousers and a tight black jacket. Father was over by the door, his head lowered to three women, speaking softly to him.

'Here, lad. You'll need to eat, whatever's happened.' A plate was thrust into my hand. On it slices of ham were piled in a mound. There was bread and cheese there too, an apple and a wedge of parkin. I found a corner and set to and didn't stop until I'd finished, not even when people pressed my shoulder and patted my head as they passed, not even when Grace and Mary Ann came and sat close beside me, not speaking. A woman pushed a cup of tea into my hand as soon as I had finished.

'Poor lamb,' she said to me as she gave it to me, and she wiped tears from my wet cheeks with her tea towel.

It was only once I'd emptied my cup that snatches of the

conversation filtered through to me. 'She was a true Samaritan, even towards the end,' said one.

'Always thinking of those worse off than herself,' chimed in another.

'Those poor motherless children, four of them living and now a baby too. Who will look after them?'

I felt a bit ashamed of eating so quickly, but I'd been hungry. I hadn't eaten much since it had happened. It was horrible. When I'd got back from the courthouse, Mother had still been upstairs with Mrs Spencer and Aunt had gone back to her, and Father had closed the shop and was in the parlour in the late-afternoon gloom, pacing, smoking his pipe which went out all the time because he didn't seem to be able to keep it in his mouth because he kept going to the bottom of the stairs and calling out, 'Hello? Hello?' to which no one answered. For hours it went on, and we all sat in the dark not moving, not speaking, watching him pacing, up and down. We held hands, and John fell asleep on Grace's lap. There were sounds from up there, and at each sound Father groaned in sympathy.

Then a silence which had stretched for an eternity.

Father froze. We sat bolt upright, not daring to speak, listening to that terrible silence.

There came the thin wail of a baby.

Silence again. Then a door opened and there were footsteps. Father raced upstairs.

We waited, for an age.

'God bless you,' Mrs Spencer came downstairs, pulling on her bonnet, then left the house. Grace bit her lip so much that I thought it would start bleeding. I didn't know what to think. Perhaps the baby had died, like the first Grace I'd never known, like Mary two years ago; she'd lived for a year, but maybe this one had died on coming into the world. It happened, I knew that. Like lots of Mary Ann's brothers and sisters.

I wasn't prepared. Father's footsteps on the stairs were heavy.

'I want Mother,' John whined, waking up.

'Yes, son, I know. We all do.' Father took his hand. 'But she is out of her suffering. We should be happy for her.'

He didn't sound happy.

'Be brave, my children. I want you to come up and see your mother.' My stomach dropped. I dreaded what I might find. I ran for the stairs and went up them two at a time. Polly jumped from step to step with me, the bell round her neck tinkling with each jump. The others weren't far behind. Aunt Patience opened the door.

'Keep that cat out,' she said, and shooed Polly away. 'Come in,' she said then, finger to her lips and we filed in silently. It was dim in the bedroom. The curtains were drawn. 'Go to your mother.'

I went over. There Mother lay, pale even against her white cotton cap and the white of the pillows. Her hand lay outside the bedclothes. I took it and gingerly climbed on to the bed.

Aunt opened her mouth to speak, but seemed to change her mind. John and Jane climbed up beside me. Grace stood silently on the other side of the bed. Mother's hand in mine felt strangely heavy. I squeezed it and waited for her to squeeze back. No such thing happened. I tried rubbing it, it felt cool. I squeezed again.

It was only then that I truly understood. Mother was gone.

Beside me, Jane set up a wailing. Grace tried to hush her, but her own lip was trembling.

'Sshh, there, there, pet,' Aunt said, holding Jane. 'Your mother is at peace. She has passed on to Heaven. But see, you have a baby sister.' She led us to the cradle. 'Her name is....' She looked up at Father. 'What are you to call the poor mite?' she asked him.

'She will be called Fanny,' he said, 'it was what my Mary wanted.'

His Mary and my mother. Mother had died. She was pretty, she loved flowers and was good to people and she sang to me. And she was dead.

Thirty

I was lying on my back still clutching a rose, my face wet, and not just with tears. I placed the rose dead centre on the Spencer grave, then hurried back along the beck in the rain.

I rang the doorbell.

No one opened the door.

I rang the bell again, heard it chime its tune. Water dripped on me from an overflowing gutter.

The door stayed shut.

I stepped back and looked to where curtains were drawn.

I waited. No one came. Was Mum with him, out of hospital? Or was he there on his own? Maybe he couldn't hear the bell from upstairs, the tune it played was so quiet.

I tried ringing once more. Then I shouted: 'Hey!' a couple of times. He'd said don't be late, and I wasn't. This wasn't fair. I *had* been back already. He was the one who hadn't been there. I picked up some gravel and aimed it at the window. It fell short. I tried again, missed again.

I beat on the door with my fist. It made no difference. I jumped from foot to foot to get warm. It was only then that I realised no car was parked outside.

What now? I had to see Mum. Twice already she'd not been

there, and now she wasn't again. No one was there, not Mum, not the gowk. In that case, I'd have to find her. I had to get to the hospital. It was somewhere the other side of Pipton, so if I could get to Pipton first, I could ask where to go.

I found Station Road and followed it to the station. A light shone down on a couple of cars parked outside; neither was the gowk's. I went through a white gate and on to the platform. No one was standing there waiting; no one was sitting on the benches. I came to the red double-door to the ticket office. No one was in; office hours were 07:15 to 16:40 said a notice. Rain hung in droplets from the two station lamps. Rain plopped into the puddles on the platform. I found a timetable in the window and read it. I'd just missed a train, and there wouldn't be another for Pipton for two hours. Back in the market square, outside the town hall, I found a man in a raincape with piercings in his nose and lip, sitting on a bench, a Labrador at his feet. 'All right?' he greeted me.

I nodded back, 'Not bad,' I answered mechanically, though it was a lie. 'Is there a bus to Pipton, do you know?'

'No good asking me, I'm just visiting,' he said. A gaggle of hikers, bent low and tired under heavy rucksacks, faces closed against the rain, went past. I reached the far corner of the square and halted because I could smell leather.

'Hurry up there, Benjamin,' came a man's voice.

I stared at the bank door. It didn't change. No one was there. But he'd told me to hurry. So I would. If I couldn't get a train or a bus, I'd have to walk. I'd need a road going the same direction as the railway line. I went under the railway bridge near the station and followed the road down and round and walked on till ahead of me I saw a main road and headlights.

Left to Pipton. There was no pavement on the main road, but here were cars. Cars flashing, wheels droning, splashing through water at the roadside coming up at me in sheets of spray. I turned and looked at one or two, hoping they'd see me and stop. No car stopped. They didn't even slow down. I trudged on, squelching through the verge. My shoes sank into the grass, and the water travelled down through my socks and began to pool under my feet. I pulled my hood up higher and walked on, concentrating on putting one foot in front of the other because eventually that would get me there. A lorry went past, its great wheels sending up a splash of water over me. The driver hooted, but didn't slow down. More cars swished past, tyres thrumming on the tarmac. I reached a bridge over the river. Still cars came, fast and furious through the rain. No one slowed, no one stopped.

There was a sudden gap in the traffic and all was still. How far was Pipton? I didn't know. How long would it take me to get there? I stopped. I didn't know where to go, not really. Maybe I was being stupid. By the time I got there, if I ever got there, Mum might even be back. I turned and retraced my steps, took the road on the right. But it wasn't the same one I'd come down; at least, I didn't think it was. There was no traffic here at all, but there were houses ahead. I trudged on, against rivulets of water running down the empty road. Through the steamed-up window of one house I saw a family at table eating; through another a woman was cooking and laughing at someone unseen; in the next, an old man in an armchair was reading the paper and a lad was staring at a laptop; the next one had its curtains drawn and blue light flickering through them which meant that they'd be watching television. Smoke climbed up from lit chimneys and I could smell coal and wood from warm houses.

A streetlight cast a yellow pool on the road and I found myself at a green that sloped up steeply, with houses jutting all around. Hadn't Mary Ann said in class that she lived past the old tannery at the Green? I could ask if her dad could take me to see Mum! He would know where the hospital was. She could come too, if she wanted.

Now the rain was coming down off the moors like curtains, one curtain sweeping across after another, and another. I headed over sodden grass to a bench under a spreading tree, to think. The tree had been planted for Queen Victoria's diamond jubilee, said a notice. That didn't impress the rooks huddled in the branches above, harshly chattering. The bench was white with their droppings. I sat on it anyway though even Mum might have told me not to, but my legs were aching and my feet. Which house was Mary Ann's? Was it the one on its own? Or one of the row at the top? I peered at them all in turn. Which door should I knock on first? I'd felt brave before, setting off, walking. I didn't feel so brave now. Maybe what I did would make no difference. Of course it could! I sat up straighter. Then I slumped again. I couldn't go knocking on all the doors till I found the right one.

What if Mum never came back? What would happen to me? I had no aunt, not like Benjamin. I could live with Kath, Mum's friend at the farm back in Wrath. Or would the gowk put me in an orphanage? My mind whirred round and round. I shivered and shook. Perhaps if I concentrated hard, if I imagined I was warm and dry, Mary Ann would sense it and come and find me. I closed my eyes.

Mary Ann was at our door, silhouetted darkly against sunshine outside. 'I wish you good day, Mr Waugh. My father's sent me to fetch Benjamin. Father says he's going to the bees, and he thought Benjamin would wish want to be there. May he come?'

'Good idea.' Father looked up from the table, his eyes red with exhaustion and grief, deep lines grooved round his mouth. 'Take John and Jane with you, lad. You go too, Grace.'

'I'll stay with you, Father, and keep you company,' Grace said.

'No, my dear.' He pushed himself up from the table. 'I must return to work. The shop cannot stay closed. Your Aunt will stay with us and take care of baby Fanny for now. Here.' From a small pile, he took a box. He thrust it into my hand and a card into Jane's. 'You can take neighbour Spencer's funeral biscuits to him, with my regards and my gratitude for taking over the bees. They cannot be kept waiting, any more than my customers. And they need to know.'

We trailed behind Mary Ann to where the hives were kept, where Mr Spencer was waiting for us.

'Now then, lad. Now then, Jane, John.' He shook our hands in turn. 'Your mother was a good woman. You can be proud of her.'

I handed him the hard sponge fingers, and Jane the black-edged card that went with them, and passed on Father's message.

'One of these will do very nicely,' he said, taking out a funeral biscuit, 'along with the ale I brought. Stand back a bit. Watch.' He lifted the top off the hive. 'You need the brood box, see, where the queen bee is.' He held his voice calm and steady.

Some bees flew up. 'They'll sting!' Jane cried.

'Hush. Happen they will and happen they won't. I'm used to it, lass.' Then he addressed the bees: 'Good morning, ma'am, good morning, bees. Your Mistress Mary Waugh is dead and William Spencer – that's me – is your new master. He sends you a bite,' he took the funeral biscuit from me, 'and a sup of ale from his table.' He dipped the finger-shaped biscuit in the ale and crumbled it over the hive, 'and he hopes you will not be offended.' Finally he took a wide strip of black cotton from his pocket and wound it around the base of the hive, before closing it again.

We listened to the subdued humming coming from inside the hive. A couple of bees flew out, buzzed around and flew back in.

'There now. They seem content, do they not? Life goes on. Be it with us as it is with them.'

We stood there, silent. Grace was the first to speak. 'I'm off home. I'll take the young ones.' Mary Ann said she had to go too, to help her mother with the wash.

A loud flapping of wings and cawing and the rooks hauled me out of the past. They rose up off the branches as if to a signal, sending twigs and wet showering down on me. I bent over and shook my head to get them out. I hunched up on the bench, crossing my hands over my chest and tucking them under my armpits for warmth and comfort. I could barely see the houses now through the sheeting rain, so wherever Mary Ann was, she probably couldn't see me either; anyway, her bedroom was likely the other side of whichever house it was she lived in. How could she know I was there? Get real!

I trudged off the Green. At the corner another road led back the way I'd come, only narrower and higher and passing along the backs of the houses below. A stench hit me full in the face, and then it subsided. But for that moment I'd smelt dung once more, and fresh, dirty hides. Now the only smell was wet stone. Further along, a building was set back. From a top window a cross shone down, electric blue. It leaned forward and seemed to sway, making me dizzy. It swayed towards me, and vanished.

The front door was opening and yellow light from a lantern splashed out. Men walked out into the night air, singly and in pairs, in black hats and long coats. They passed me at the ornamental iron gate, calling goodnight to one another but not to me.

I stayed there till one man was left alone in the door opening. He snuffed the lamp, closed the door and locked it, and trudged down the path. He looked tireder and older, the way he had since Mother died, but when he saw me his grave face relaxed. 'Now then, our Benjamin. Have you come to fetch me home? Are the young 'uns having their supper?'

'Grace is seeing to them.'

'She's a good lass. And you're a good lad.' He sighed. 'We need to think about your future and your education, and Grace's and Jane's.' He slung an arm about my shoulders; it lay there heavy and warm and we began to pick our way down the steep hill in the darkness. 'Only not yet,' he muttered to himself, 'not yet.'

'In you go, lad,' said Father, opening our heavy oak door. I turned to smile at him.

I was smiling at no one, and the feeling of warmth on my shoulder was going. I was on the corner, and there was no leather smell, just the bank behind. My head span. One moment I was here, the next there. Mother was dead and Father was talking about my future. Mum was in hospital and I didn't know why. My worlds were turning into one; which did I really belong to?

Thirty-one

I waited in case I slipped backwards again. I even tried the door to the bank in case it changed, or let me in; it was shut and locked with a modern lock. Apart from a couple leaving the pub, and a car that sprayed puddles at me, the square was deserted. I sloshed down through the wet, back to the river, my trainers squelching with every step. It was the colour of milk and chocolate and it bubbled and raged, leaped and danced at me, as if it wanted to wash me off the bridge. Somehow that brought me to my senses. 'You can't get me!' I taunted.

At the house there was still no car. No light showed from any window. I rang the bell again, I threw stones again, just in case. Outside the post office café I paused, wondering about knocking on the door with its Closed sign, but it was dark now and late and I mightn't be so welcomed this time.

Where to? Headlights caught my face as a car swung round the bend, blinding me for a moment. I watched it, in case it went to the house, but it swished on past the beck, leaving the street deserted once more. I ran back to the churchyard, down the gravestone path to the church porch and sat on the stone seat where I'd been with the other Mary Ann for the funeral, where the vicar had found me. Maybe I'd find an answer there.

But the stone was as cold as a tomb, and the silence of the porch and what might be on the other side of the great oak door spooked me, that and the rain thudding down outside, and I pelted out, past the row of crooked cottages gleaming white, shoes slapping on the ancient stones of the high pavement. Left, past a bigger house. Left again at the stony track, running, running, a stitch stabbing my side. Water streaked down the pitted surface of the courtyard; it gushed from a broken pipe beside the cellar doors. I went straight to them, and pushed. One side creaked open and I stepped inside. Something sounded behind me, like the fall of a foot, and I turned. Nothing and no one. I took another step. Again I heard something behind. I turned. Nothing. I went in further. Perhaps it was just the echo of my own footsteps.

Behind me, the cellar door slammed shut.

My throat dried. My heart banged against my ribs. I whimpered, I couldn't help it. I was trapped between whatever might be behind me and whatever could be waiting ahead in the solid darkness.

Nothing happened. Nothing was here, just me, and the strange shapes in the darkness around. I stood still, waiting, in case anything moved. As my eyes adjusted, I made out the shadowy edges of jutting-out stones, of large hooks, of wooden beams. I shook water off me like a dog, and took off my shoes. I stretched out my arms and began groping my way, hand over hand on dusty stone, treading carefully, towards the far chamber.

There was something in the corner. I reached out. When all I touched was rough sacking, my shoulders relaxed. At least in here it was dry. At least here I was sheltered. By now I was shivering violently like an engine, and it was difficult to tug out one sack, but I managed, and did my best to dry myself on it. Then I tugged out another and wrapped it around me, and sank down on the pile of the other sacks. It was even warm there from a hot pipe that ran along the wall beside me. Above, I could hear footsteps and running water and the whisper of music. A man and woman were talking, but their words were muffled.

The darkness wrapped itself around me and I curled up, resting my head on my arm.

There was a tapping, a rapping. There came the sound of hands beating on stone. Someone was hammering on the floor, from underneath.

I scrambled away from the sacks till I was squashed up against the wall. Bile rose in my throat.

''et me ou'!' The words were muffled. It was dark! How could I know what would be under there?

''et me ou'!'

I put my hands over my ears.

'-eease!' It was louder.

I swallowed hard. I crept forward. The cries must be coming from under the slab I'd investigated before. I remembered the smells, of sweat, of fear. I was shaking. But I had to find out what was under there. Or who. 'OK, OK. I'll help,' I whispered, and it sounded like a promise.

I crawled over the stone floor. The slabs felt solid, until I found the one that rocked. I knelt on the side of the slab and pressed.

But it wasn't stone, it was a trapdoor, made of wood. Weirdly, I could see quite clearly now. There was an iron bolt on it and an iron ring. I was kneeling beside it, my woollen trousers rough against my knees.

'Le' me out!' The words were clearer now, but croaky, panicky.

The bolt was stiff. At last I drew it open. I tried lifting the trapdoor, but it was heavy. 'Push from your side!' I called.

Silence.

So I put both hands to the great iron ring and pulled with all my might. The trapdoor thudded over, and I tumbled backwards with it. I righted myself quickly and looked down.

The face that looked up at me from dark steps was skinny and drawn and smudged and scared. And familiar.

We stared at each other. 'You! What're you doing there, Morphet?'

He struggled to get out. But he was weak, so I stretched out my hands and hoisted him up. 'You forgot to give me food,' he accused me.

I put my hand to my mouth. He was right. I'd not thought of him for days, because of Mother dying and the new baby. I'd almost forgotten him. 'But why are you here?'

'Father put me in. Said I could die here, for all he cared.'

'Why didn't you get out below?' At the bottom of the steps was a tiny space, and a door. You could get out there on to a path at the back without being seen and cut through to the graveyard and escape. I knew because I'd played here with my friends.

'He blocked up the door so I couldn't. He said....' Morphet gulped. 'He said he'd be safer with me locked up. An' I could die for all he cared. I'm starving, Benjamin.' He was sobbing as if his heart would pour out on the stones.

I pulled him down on to the sacks and wrapped my arm round him and rocked him, to try to stop him shuddering.

Slowly his sobbing quietened.

'But why did he do that, Morphet? What happened?'

He shook his head.

'Tell me,' I urged. 'Trust me.'

'I stole penny buns from the baker. It weren't the first time.'

I gasped. 'You what? But- they'll-'

'I know, but you'd forgot me. I had nowt. Father catched me. He said I were lucky it were him. He said if the baker'd catched me this time they'd hang me. He didn't care. 'Cept that he'd be blamed along with me and hanged with me. Or else they'd send him to Australy. 'Sides, he'd be short without my turd money. He were raging like I've not seen. He put me in the pigsty. When dark came he strapped me to a wheelbarrow and dumped rubbish and all sorts on me and brung me here and locked me up. For ever, he said. He didn't want me.'

The words jerked out. I tried to absorb what he'd told. It was my fault. I'd promised the magistrate.

'Give us summat to eat, our Benjamin.'

'I will,' I promised. 'I'll fetch it.'

'No, I'll not stay here!' He clutched at me. 'Take me with you.'

Thirty-two

'Well, well, you again. A stowaway now, are you?'

I jerked awake. Dr Gabriel was crouching beside me. 'Hello there. I thought you'd never wake up. You're trespassing, you know,' she said sternly.

'I haven't stolen anything,' I blurted out.

'Did I say you had?' She looked bemused. 'Have you been here all night?'

I felt chilled and stiff. I looked around as I struggled to sit up, but no one else was on the sacks. She seemed to be talking only to me. 'I couldn't get in.'

'Get in where?'

Morphet had been shut in. I'd been shut out. I swallowed hard and tried to concentrate on what she'd asked. She was waiting for an answer.

'In the house. He wasn't there to let me in.'

'Wasn't he? And who would "he" be?'

I stared down at my knees, frowning, remembering Morphet and my promise. No! I shook my head to free it of that memory.

'Who would he be?' she repeated. 'Were you running away? Is this your luggage?' She pointed at my bag.

I shook my head. 'It's my school bag.'

'Ah. And what time should you be at school?'

'By nine o'clock.' I struggled to my feet. School. Me, Percy. That was reality.

'I see. Well, it's eight o'clock now. Can you smell bacon?'

I could; it had wafted into the cellar with her.

'Come and have breakfast with us, then off to school with you. Tell me where you live and I'll let them know you're all right. They'll be worrying.'

'They won't.' I wouldn't look her in the eyes.

'Oh, really? Why's that?'

'He doesn't care. And Mum's in hospital. And he won't let me see her.' A tear trickled down my cheek, then another, and another. I couldn't stop them. I didn't want to cry!

She regarded me from cool, grey eyes. 'Will she be there for long?'

'I don't know,' I snuffled.

'Where do you live? Where's home?'

'It isn't home, don't call it that!' I knuckled my eyes to stop the tears, scrubbed my cheeks hard with my knuckles.

She looked concerned. 'All right, calm down. Where does she live when she isn't in hospital? Is it here in Seggleswick?'

'Yes,' I said through gritted teeth. 'Along the beck. At Mr Bockley's.'

She stood up. 'Right. We'd better go upstairs before Thomas eats all the breakfast on his own. I was coming down for wood for the stove; he'll be wondering what's keeping me. Will you come with me?' She held out a hand.

I hung back. 'What about Morphet?' I said urgently.

She looked puzzled. 'Morphet? Now there's an odd old-fashioned name. What about him? I can't see any Morphet.'

I got to my feet, feeling stupid.

'Upstairs. Come on.' She hesitated, then added, 'Come upstairs, Ben Bockley.'

'Waugh,' I said fiercely. 'It's not Bockley.'

She started. 'Ben Waugh? Well, well. Who'd have thought it!'

Thirty-three

'Percy, a word.' Mr Magnus beckoned me over in the playground at break. 'I've just been speaking to your….' He stopped himself just in time. 'Tell me, where did you spend last night?'

I wouldn't catch his eye.

'Hmm. Mr Bockley rang. He's worried about you. It appears that you ran away from home.'

'I didn't run away, and it's not home! He shut me out.'

'Hush. He says that you spent the night in a cellar. He says a woman called on him this morning and told him that she'd found you there.'

'He's lying!'

'Percy.' He tapped his fingers on his cheek thoughtfully and looked over his glasses at me. 'It's a serious matter to accuse someone of lying.'

I stared at my feet.

'Come now. Which part might have been untrue? Let's sit down and start again, mmm?' He sat on the nearby bench and patted the seat beside him. 'There, that's better. Now – did you run away?'

I shook my head. 'He wasn't there. He'd told me not to be

late, and I wasn't, but he wasn't there. I couldn't get in. He wouldn't have worried, he doesn't care, he...'

'All right.' He raised a hand to stop me. 'It sounded to me as if he cared. He told me he couldn't sleep for worrying. It was rather unfortunate, he says. He went to a colleague's for supper and then on to see your mother in hospital, and he was late getting back, and he forgot to phone you.'

'He never told me about going to any supper.'

'So I gather.' Mr Magnus twiddled his pen in his hand.

'How was I to know he'd be late? Anyway, I haven't got a phone. He knows that.'

'What about the cellar; did you spend the night in a cellar?'

I blinked furiously.

'Did you?' he repeated, gently.

'Yes.'

'And is it true that you're not eating breakfast?'

'I had breakfast this morning. Liz gave it me.'

'Liz?'

'The cellar woman.'

'And has this Liz another name?'

I nodded. 'Dr Gabriel.'

'Dr Gabriel! What about yesterday? I don't think you had breakfast yesterday either, did you?'

I was startled. How did he know?

'Mary Ann.' He beckoned.

I turned in surprise. I hadn't realised that she was hovering behind.

'Will you take Percy home with you after school? I've asked your father, and he's agreed.'

'Yes, Uncle Mag.'

Uncle Mag? My mouth dropped open.

'While we see what's to be done.' Mr Magnus wrinkled his nose at me. 'Don't look so surprised. I'm her uncle, can't you see the resemblance?'

Mary Ann was laughing at the expression on my face.

'Her father is my brother. But at school I'm Mr Magnus, just as I am to you.'

'You can take me to the hospital, can't you?'

'We'll see. I need to make some enquiries first.'

'Will you come to ours then?' said Mary Ann.

Her face blurred, the playground turned black and span around me. That's when I fainted.

'Are you coming to us for your tea, our Benjamin?' Mary Ann was at the door to her house in Kirkgate.

I lowered the wheelbarrow.

'What's in there?'

'Nothing much.'

'Oh?' She came over and twitched the sacking.

'Don't!'

'Why, Benjamin? What're you hiding? Where are you going?'

I had to stop her questions in case any passersby decided to halt and listen. 'I'm going home. You can come, if you like.'

'But what's in there?' She closed the house door behind her and joined me.

'Hush your voice, and I'll tell you.'

I did, as we crossed the square, only stopping speaking when anyone came close. '...So I copied Morphet's father,' I finished. 'There was a wheelbarrow in the barn next to the cellar. It's Morphet in there, under the sacks.'

When we got to the shop it was empty, apart from Father, hanging a bunch of reins from a hook in the ceiling. He stared at us as we wheeled the barrow right into the shop.

'Shut the door, Mary Ann,' I told her.

'What are you doing?' Father dropped the reins on the counter and tried to stop her. 'I have a business to run. It isn't closing time yet.'

'Wait. Look, Father.' I lifted off the sacking.

Morphet staggered out of the barrow and stood, bowed, beside it.

'What is this all about? Benjamin, explain.'

When I was finished, Father rubbed his tired eyes. 'This is a serious matter, my boy. Baker Ingham runs a decent business, as do I. We are honest folk in this town. We support one another; you know that. Theft cannot be tolerated.'

I nodded. 'But it was only two penny buns, Father, and it was my fault he did it. I can pay for them from my money box. It wasn't his fault! I promised he'd not go hungry, and then I forgot.'

'In which case you share the blame, do you not. But it remains a crime. "Thou shalt not steal".'

'But Father: "Feed my lambs!"' I retorted.

'I am glad to see that you know your Bible so well,' he said drily. Then he was silent. Mary Ann didn't move. Nor did Morphet. Nor did I.

At last he spoke. 'The boy has a father. He has a home of his own to go to.'

'There is no food there!' I took a huge breath. 'Mother wouldn't sent him back! She would have wanted me to look after him.'

Father looked shocked. 'Your mother was a good woman, the best. But you do not know what she would have done, and it is not your place to lecture me.' He paused then said, 'Very well, take him through and ask Grace to give him a bowl of porridge. Then put him in your bed; you can share tonight. We'll see what to do in the morning.'

Thirty-four

They'd taken me to the staffroom when I'd fainted, and that's where I came round. Mary Ann was with me. When, shortly afterwards, we came out of school a man was waiting for us, tall, with high, sharp cheekbones like Mr Magnus, but with hair almost as fair as Mary Ann's. I stood back as he bent to kiss her. 'You must be Percy,' he said then, shaking my hand, 'good to have you aboard.'

'Dad, can we show P the chapel?'

'And there I was, thinking you'd like to have tea and cake at Poppies on the way home, as a treat. But fine, chapel it is.'

'Da-ad!' Mary Ann danced around him. 'We can have cake on the way, can't we? P hasn't had any cake for *weeks*!'

'Have you not?'

I shook my head.

'And he fainted today, in lunch break.'

'Yes, Mary Ann, I heard. We'd better remedy that then, hadn't we,' and he took us to the café. We didn't have tea at all; we had hot chocolate and curd tart at a blue table with baskets and dried flowers hanging from the ceiling, and for a while that took everything else from my head.

'I have to pick my shoes up on the way. I'll only be a tick,' he said down by the post office and crossed the road to a shop on the other side. Nelson Footwear, it said over the door.

Nelson footwear: a cobbler. A wooden money box, pennies for the poor.

'Hey, P!' Mary Ann clicked her fingers at me. 'Are you all right? You've gone all funny.'

I tore my eyes away from the sign. 'Yeh, I'm fine.'

Up we walked past the Folly, on up the steep hill; the road was becoming familiar. There was the iron gate and the chapel. Now in daylight, there was no cross blazing, but you could just make out its shape in an upstairs window. We were going up the short path to the chapel. 'Are *you* going to take me to see Mum?' I asked Mary Ann's father.

'We're finding out what's best to do.'

I bit my lip. I'd wait then, for now. If he didn't, and no one else would, I'd make sure I got there myself, somehow.

He took out his key and unlocked the door and in we went.

I knew the place! Rows of polished pews facing front. Shiny white iron columns reaching up to a circular balcony. And the ceiling was blue, as blue as the sky at twilight.

In front of us was a table and, behind it, the pulpit. It seemed to beckon me. I went forward and mounted the few steps. Behind me, Mary Ann tittered. When I got to the pulpit and looked down she and her father were sitting below in a pew, arms folded, looking expectantly at me. My congregation. I could see that Mary Ann was trying hard not to laugh.

'Are you going to give us a sermon, young man?' asked her father.

There was a roaring and a rushing in my eyes and in my ears and I opened my mouth:

'...I was an hungred and ye gave me meat, naked and ye clothed me, a stranger and ye took me in...'

My voice was deep, the voice of a grown man. Below me the pews were filled with people; they were so full that more were standing at the back to hear me too, packed in like herrings.

Mary Ann was on her feet. 'Are you going to faint again, P? You're going all peculiar. Your mouth's opening and closing like a goldfish.'

'I expect he's hungry,' said her father, looking concerned, too. 'One curd tart clearly wasn't enough.'

I shut my mouth, dazed. The pulpit rail was up to my chest. When I'd been speaking it had been below me, as if I had been taller, like a man.

'Come down from there!' Mary Ann urged.

My legs wobbled as I left the pulpit, trailing my hand along the rail.

'Mary Ann's going to help me get the cups and saucers ready for tonight's meeting,' her father said. 'Sit quietly, or wander about, as you like.' He started humming a tune.

I froze. 'What's that?'

'What's what?'

'What you're humming.'

'Oh. Just something from *The Messiah*.'

That confused me all over again. I'd heard Mother singing the same words. Now it wasn't so much that I was turning up in some other place as that some other place was coming up and echoing where I was now. I tried to fathom it out as I sat there and waited.

As we left the iron gate and were back on the road,

something made me look back. A man in a black overcoat was opening the chapel door and going in. He turned and looked at me. It was Father.

And then he was gone. Mary Ann hadn't seen. Her father hadn't seen. She chattered all the way up to the Green. She didn't notice the stench blasting out from the house where I knew the tannery had been. It didn't make her stomach turn the way it did mine. She didn't notice how quiet I was being.

When we reached the Green, they led me to the house that stood alone. It had once been a barn, they told me. Now where cattle must have lain on straw in winter, there were books. Books were crammed on to shelves, scattered carelessly on window sills, tottering in piles on the floor, tossed on sofas that sagged like ours had at home, bright rugs thrown over them. A fire was lit and a labrador lay sprawled on the hearthrug. It lifted its head and shambled to its feet to approach Mary Ann. She met it halfway and knelt and buried her head in its fur. 'This is Punter,' she said, 'he's almost as old as I am. Punter, meet P, P meet Punter.'

'When you've finished, Mary Ann, I need you and Percy to clear the table and as soon as your brother's in, we'll eat.' Her father winked at me. 'I may be untidy but I'm a dab hand in the kitchen. Cottage pie suit you?'

'And then you'll take me to see Mum?' But he had his back to me and was already busy getting ready to cook.

When Mary Ann's brother came back from rugby, her father put cottage pie on the table and we pulled up our chairs. Steam rose from it when he dug in the spoon, and a rich gravy smell. When we'd finished every last bit of it, even the crusts of potato stuck round the top edges, Mary Ann's father got out packs of cards and taught us Racing Demon, and I never wanted the day to end.

Mr Magnus our teacher walked in. He watched us finish the hand. 'I've a surprise,' he said. 'For you, Percy. Your mother's back. I've come to fetch you.'

I jumped to my feet, scattering cards like confetti. 'Where is she?'

'At…' He broke off, but I knew what he meant all right. 'I'm taking you back there.'

Thirty-five

'Percy.' Mum held out her arms to me and I ran into them. 'Oh, how I've missed you. Thank you for bringing him,' she said to Mr Magnus, 'that was kind of you.' Her voice vibrated against my head. She was warm and she wasn't dead.

'I trust he hasn't been a nuisance.' The gowk spoke.

'A nuisance? Not at all.' A hand ruffled my hair. 'I'll be going then. I wonder, Mrs Waugh, might we have a word tomorrow? Perhaps when you come to meet Percy after school?'

A pause. I turned round within the safety of Mum's arms and watched Mr Magnus.

'Yes, of course.'

'Good. Well, I'll wish you all a good night,' and he was gone.

The minute the door closed behind Mr Magnus, the gowk smiled awkwardly at me. Then he pointed at my feet. 'Shoes.'

I didn't go, not at first. 'Mary Ann took me to hers, Mum, and we had cottage pie and we played cards and she's got a brother and her father's…'

'Hold it right there. Shoes.' Then he tried to sound all hearty once I'd dumped them. 'Well, what have you been up to that your teacher needs to see us?'

'Nothing. And he didn't say he wanted to speak to you, he

said Mum.' Mum had been away for days and I hadn't seen her and all he wanted to do was tell me to take off my shoes and imply I'd not been behaving myself at school! What about the night before? He didn't mention that.

His mouth opened and closed again, but no sound came out. He cleared his throat, and spoke at last. 'Shouldn't you be in bed? It's past your bedtime. Off you go.' He pointed upstairs.

Mum frowned. 'Ian….' She caught me to her again and squeezed me, as if she'd never let go. But she did. 'All right. Go on, love, go on up. I'll be up in a tick.'

'Can you think why the teacher wants to see me?' she was asking him as I was almost at the top stair.

He hesitated before answering. 'I expect the boy's done something wrong. Or it could be because he stayed out all night. He spent it in some woman's cellar. She may have told the school.'

I hovered, listening.

'He did what? A cellar?' I could hear shock in her voice. 'Why would he do such a thing?'

'I omitted to tell Percy that after visiting you in hospital, I'd be having supper with the district manager and his wife, and I wasn't back at the usual-'

'You omitted!' she interrupted. 'He's only a young lad. You should have put him first.'

'I skipped coffee once I realised, and came straight home.'

'Oh, well done.' She had her sarcastic-cross voice on.

I lay down on the landing and peered down through the railings.

'He never turned up. He should have waited.'

'It was pouring last night!'

'Well, so I imagined he'd have found shelter. He's an intelligent boy.'

'Exactly. A boy, Ian, not an adult. And anyway – you imagined? Did you go looking for him?'

'How was I to know where he'd be? Don't go on so. I expected he'd go to a friend, or find shelter somewhere. You're always saying how proud you are of his resilience, his independence. Besides, he should have left me a note, my love.'

'Don't you my love me; this is my son we're talking about!' There was another note in her voice, one I hadn't heard for a long time. 'I don't think I want to hear this, Ian.' Footsteps crossed the room. Quick as a flash I went and climbed into bed, not even going first to the bathroom to clean my teeth.

Mum came up. 'Numkin.' She bundled me up in my duvet and cuddled me close. 'I'd stay for us to catch up, but there are things to discuss with Ian that won't keep. Then we'll have a good long talk. Soon, I promise. I'll look in again later.'

I waited for her for a while, listening to his rumbling; he seemed to be doing a lot of talking. I wondered what else he was saying about me. There wasn't much of an answering murmur from Mum.

Had anything changed after all, I wondered, dolefully punching my pillow into shape and lying back.

I didn't want to fall asleep, not until she came back. But I did.

When I'd woken, there'd been only me in my bed, and only John in John's. I went downstairs and found Grace in the kitchen stirring the porridge, and an empty bowl in the sink. Father was in the shop preparing to open up. There was no sign of Morphet.

'I took him back. And before you start in,' Father raised a hand, 'I'll have no arguing. You promised the magistrate you'd make sure Morphet is fed. He had porridge this morning before I took him back.'

'We can give him a home!'

'Benjamin, he has a home. He has a father. We cannot just take him in like that. I have spoken to Mr Bibber and said that he must take better care of his own, that we'd be watching. Now. Will you help in the shop today?'

I didn't. Instead I went off with my friends to the moors, to Catbells Foss because the day was warm and it could be our last chance to swim before winter, and I was cross with Father. We scrambled over slippery rocks, stripped off and plunged into the cold, rust-coloured pool. We shot back to the surface like corks and swam to where the waterfall cascaded down from the moor above, taking it in turn to let its force pound our head and shoulders. Way above us the late autumn sun slanted and sparkled through the leaves of tall trees, rooted in the sides of the hollow leading to the pool. We fooled around, swam, dived, heading always back to the mighty waterfall, daring it, the pounding, beating in my ears, removing all thoughts from my mind.

We walked down off the moors, whistling.

'Eh, what's going on there?'

People were clustering in a knot at the tenement building.

Screams were coming from inside, then silence, and the silence was worse than the screaming, especially with the thudding that we could hear. Until all the sound stopped.

People drifted away. My friends drifted away. A door

opencd and Morphet's father lurched out, tightening his belt. He belched as he passed me, and in the belch were all the smells of hell.

Then I knew what had happened. I ran inside. Morphet was in the corner on the floor, bleeding.

Thirty-six

When I came down in the morning and before I sat down, the gowk cleared his throat. 'Erm. Percy.' He looked at Mum. 'I owe you an apology.'

I didn't know what to say.

'Why don't you ask a friend round after school?' Mum suggested. 'That Mary Ann. Or Harry, or – the boy with the odd name, Morphet, was it?'

Before I could answer, he'd butted in. 'I'm not sure… I mean, things might get…'

'Broken? Just because I broke a jug. It's all right, Mum, I won't bother.'

Mum pursed her lips, and that was that and we got on with breakfast.

In fact when I got to school, Mary Ann wasn't in class anyway, and Daniel was sent to another table to help Kyle and I was left on my own with Louise who ignored me.

'How many hours in a year?' asked Mr Magnus

'Two thousand nine hundred and sixty?' said Louise.

'Is she right? Come on, come on, is she right? No, you don't need your calculators for this. Think!'

Mr Magnus was short with us, and became irritated when

we began to give answers that he thought were silly. 'There's too much noise in here. Who can hear themselves think?'

No one put up their hand.

'Exactly. We're getting visitors today from the high school and it'll be embarrassing for me if there's chaos and anarchy in here, so buck up.'

It was that kind of day. Mr Magnus made no reference to Mum.

Daniel told me at lunch that Mary Ann had had to go to Leeds and he and Harry and I had lunch together, but I hardly spoke. Mum was back but what difference did it make?

When I came out of school she wasn't there to meet me after all. But as I reached the footbridge over the river, I heard running footsteps behind. 'Percy! Wait!' She was red in the face, and panting.

'Are you all right? Mum? Are you having a heart attack?'

'No, you dafty. I just need to catch my breath. There, that's better. We have to talk, just the two of us. Not in the house. We'll go to a café for tea.'

Poppies was full with a big group and Mum said we had to talk seriously and needed a table to ourselves so we went to the post office café.

'Good afternoon,' said the café owner to Mum when we were settled at the window in the tiny café-shop. There was no one else in there. 'What would you like? And you, young man, crumpets and ginger beer like last time?'

Mum looked startled. 'Last time?'

'Oh, he's quite a regular,' he said, though it wasn't true.

'Does that mean you've been shut out more than the once?'

Mum asked quietly when he had moved away.

'Well, he locks everything and I'm not allowed a key, so how can I get in if you're not there?'

'Ssh. Keep your voice down. In this place secrets fly round town and get halfway to Carlisle if you're not careful.' But the owner had gone through to the kitchen and was out of hearing, and no one else was there. 'But at night, I mean. Is it just the once you've been in a cellar?'

As if that wasn't enough! I nodded.

She stared into space. A nerve at the side of her eye twitched. 'I must say,' she said, changing the subject. 'I do like it here with this fire blazing even if it isn't properly cold yet, and what pretty geraniums.' She pointed to them in the window box on the other side of the window, as if I hadn't seen them for myself. She read the menu: 'Apple crumble and ice cream, jam rolypoly, treacle rolypoly, spotted dick. Yum. Why are we just having crumpets?' She didn't seem to be able to stop talking. 'I thought we could do this, go to a café, once a week, just the two of us.'

'Mum.'

'You'd like that, wouldn't you? And you can choose the café. We can go to a different one each time.'

'All right.' I didn't care where we went so long as I was with her. 'Mum.' I bit my lip hard. 'Mum, are you really really not going to die?'

I waited for her to answer. She put down the menu. 'Did you think I was dying? My poor numkin.' She gave me an almighty hug. 'I'm so sorry. No, of course I'm not. At least, not until you're years and years older and I'm ancient. I've got some weird virus that kept them guessing for a while. It makes me tired, but that will pass.'

'You're not pregnant either?'

'You thought that, too?' She shook her head, smiling. 'Well, I'm not.'

'He wouldn't let me come and see you!' I burst out.

Her face clouded. 'Yes, I know, and that must have been horrid for you. But to be fair, pet, he works near the hospital, and it wouldn't have been convenient for him to come back to fetch you.'

Convenient! That was the gowk's word. I pulled away from her.

She sighed. 'So how was your day at school?'

'It was OK. Mum, let's go home.'

She didn't respond.

'Please, Mum.'

Her eyes roamed over my face. It was as if she could see right inside me. 'Don't you want to hear what your teacher said?' she said at last.

'I've done nothing wrong!'

'We weren't talking about your behaviour or your school work. He was worried about you spending the night in a cellar. Mr Magnus told me that the people who own the cellar gave you breakfast. He's been talking to them. I'd like to meet them, too, and thank them. He also says that you have a lively imagination.'

'I don't make things up!'

'Percy – I realise that things haven't been easy for you.' She fiddled with her teaspoon. 'Ian does mean well, you know.'

'He hates me. You should hear him when you're not there.'

Her eyes searched my face, her head tilted. 'We have to make changes,' she went on slowly.

'So we'll go home?'

''No, but things will be different. I'll need your help.'

What was it that she was going to ask? What other changes were there that would matter?

'We need a family conference,' she raised a hand to stop me pointing out that we weren't a family, 'and I want you there. We have to sort things out.'

But all I wanted was for us to be gone.

'Take that look off your face!' She began laughing. 'You should just see yourself! Go on, have a look.'

I got up and went to the mirror above the range, making sure that my expression didn't change on the way.

'See? You look as if you've swallowed a toad and have woven your eyebrows into a knot.'

As I glanced in the café mirror I saw what she meant. Because she was still laughing and I hadn't heard her laugh for ages and ages, I pretended to spit out a toad.

And there he was, right at my shoulder. He had on a woollen jacket and his hair was longer than mine but his eyes were my own forget-me-not blue. I knew that if I turned that he wouldn't be there. 'Come here, Mum,' I said, barely moving my lips. I wanted to show her. I kept my eyes on him, because I knew too that if I looked away, he would vanish.

She came and put an arm round me and leaned her head against mine in the mirror, blocking him out.

He was gone. 'Did you see?'

'Mmm?' She smiled at my reflection.

'Did you see him, in the mirror?'

'I saw me, and I saw you. No one else.'

Thirty-seven

Back at the house, I went upstairs and stared in the bedroom mirror. I put both hands on the glass and willed and willed the reflection to come again.

It didn't. But my shoulder dipped and I smelled a familiar stink. There I was, supporting Morphet, and we were staggering in the back door, to the kitchen.

Grace gasped as we came in when she saw Morphet, and the blood on him and the way he was leaning on me. 'I'll fetch Father.'

'Don't! Father mustn't see him.'

Morphet was shaking his head too, as his eyes ranged round the room, haunted.

Grace watched as I set Morphet down on a chair. She filled a bowl with water and took it over and sponged the blood away, gently, murmuring to him all the while as if he was a wild animal. Then to me, quietly, she said, 'Why not? Father can help.'

'He sent him back to Amos Bibber before. He'd do it again.'

'He wouldn't. Not when he sees this, not Father. He's just, and fair.' She frowned. 'Even so, how can Morphet come and live with us, Benjamin? We'll be off to Uncle John's school in the south in a week's time, you and me and Jane.' To board with Uncle and a few other scholars. 'Morphet won't have you here in the house to look after him then. You'd only be able to in the holidays.'

'Workhouse,' Morphet muttered.

'What?' We'd been talking over his head.

'I want to go to the workhouse.'

'The workhouse! But that's for…'

'Folk like me,' Morphet said. 'That's right. But I'd be away from him.' He spat out the word. 'I'd have food. I'd have a place to sleep. I'd have clothes.'

Grace and I looked at one another. 'You're right,' I said finally. 'Fetch Father.'

Father was on the board of guardians of the workhouse.

By the time the gowk got back, we were perched on the high stools at the kitchen table, waiting. Mum had poured out apple juice before asking me to be quiet while she gathered her thoughts.

'Well, well,' he said, coming in. He put his keys in the bureau drawer and hung up his coat in its usual place, tugged at his suit jacket, smoothed down his hair and went and hugged Mum. Still with his arm around her, he faced me across the table. 'This is unusual, you both here at the table when I come home. I really am sorry, you know. About the other night.'

I ducked my head.

'Anyway. I'm glad to see you, my boy.'

Mum put out a hand to stop me saying that I wasn't his boy. Anyway, for once I was glad to see him, too, because I wanted to hear what Mum had in mind.

She took a deep breath and started. 'I did a lot of thinking when I was in hospital. Oh, sit down, Ian.'

He looked startled at her almost-order. 'I think we should have tea, don't you? I'm sure Percy would like a cup too.'

But she didn't get up to fill the kettle as he expected. 'Please, sit. We need to talk.' She pushed a glass of juice over to him.

Grrghum, he cleared his throat. 'Surely we said all that had to be said last night.'

'No. You talked, I listened. It's my turn now.'

He sighed. 'Very well. What is it?'

'I went to see Mr Magnus, as he asked.'

'Ah yes. And what has Percival been up to?'

'Percy hasn't been "up to" anything. We had a good talk, and it helped firm up what I've been slow to acknowledge.' She took a deep breath. 'Things haven't been quite right, have they? We have to face up to that. Percy spending the night in a cellar is just the tip of the iceberg. There have to be changes – starting with me trying harder to find work – any kind.' It came out in a rush.

'Of course. But what's the rush? The doctor said you have to take things easy.'

'I've been taking things easy ever since Percy and I moved in with you and that didn't stop me getting sick, did it?'

'There isn't actually any need for you to work. I've enough to support us.'

'Just a part-time job, which will give me time with Percy.' She wasn't asking, she was telling him.

'Percy.' He turned to me, taking control. 'This isn't a conversation for your ears. Will you either go outside, or to your room.'

'No, love. Stay here.' Mum put her hand over mine. I looked from one to the other. 'Don't try to talk me out of it, Ian. What I have to say concerns Percy too. Mr Magnus says although there are no teaching vacancies there at the moment, I've a pretty good chance of getting a job for now as teaching assistant at the school.'

'Mr Magnus this, Mr Magnus that. How could you discuss this with Mr Magnus before asking me!' Sweat beaded his forehead and I didn't think it was from the warmth of the kitchen. 'Look, I agree that we have to make changes. In the light of that, I've been making enquiries myself. There's an excellent school up the road that takes boarders. He could come home at weekends, if necessary. If it were just the two of us… It would be even better if only Percy…'

'Wasn't here, too? Is that what you were trying to say? But Percy is here, Ian, and he's my son.'

'Of course he's your son. I'm well aware that this is where the problem lies.'

A problem. That's what I was, a problem.

'Ian, Ian, stop right there. It's all right, love, relax.' She gripped my hand as if to stop me running off.

'I would be able to meet the fees in full. So you'd have no need to worry about that.'

'I wasn't. Percy belongs here with me. I'd *like* to work. I need my own life, you see, Ian.'

A vein bulged and began throbbing on his forehead. I didn't want to be in on the conversation any longer. The walls were closing in on me. 'Can I go out?'

Mum gave me one of her long looks. 'All right, but don't go far, will you?' She kissed me on the forehead.

I picked up my shoes and ran for the graveyard. I pounded down the flat gravestones of the path, reading the names of those whose bones lay below: Dixon, Hargreaves, Nicholson, Harger, chanting them out loud, trying to calm my breathing. It was like being a yoyo, up one minute with Mum's plans, down the next when he came with plans of his own. About me. I went and sat on the grass of the Spencer grave. I should have stayed! He'd get Mum to change her mind, he was clever at that. I felt sick inside. I leaned against the broad tombstone. In a moment I'd go back, in a moment. I closed my eyes.

'What are you doing there?'

I opened my eyes. Mary Ann was right in front of me in a grey dress, her pigtails tied with black ribbon, stout black boots on her feet.

'You'll have dirt all over your trousers when you get up. The grass over Agnes hasn't grown over properly yet.' She was bent over, peering at me, her hands planted on her knees. 'Are you all right? You've cut your hair or something. Benjamin?'

Woollen trousers prickled my legs as I shifted on hard soil. A blackbird flew across my eyes, almost crashing into me. I pulled up my knees. The world whirled.

'You do look peculiar.'

So would Mary Ann have looked peculiar if the world had spun in front of her as it had in front of me. Twice. And if the same person was talking to me with a bit of a different voice. The Mary Ann who'd suddenly appeared in her pinafore and boots was gone and in her place was Mary Ann in jeans and jumper, her straw-coloured hair now in a plait with a blue and red spotted ribbon.

Perhaps I was going peculiar, mad. Switching like that again so quickly, back and forth. You heard of people losing their minds. Perhaps I was losing mine.

'Percy!' It was Mum calling in the street. 'Percy! Where are you?'

I scrambled to my feet. 'Here!'

'So is this where you come.' She came through the churchyard, looking round at the graves.

'Meet Mary Ann, Mum,' I said quickly.

'Hello, Mary Ann. Percy, I need more time, you know, to talk to him.' She didn't seem to want to name him in front of an outsider.

Mary Ann looked uncertain. 'I'll go, shall I?'

'No, don't. I'm sorry, I didn't mean to be rude. It's good to meet a friend of Percy's.'

I grinned suddenly, realising three things. One, she'd been there when I came out of school – well, nearly. Two, she'd come looking for me and she'd found me. Three, she'd met Mary Ann.

'P came to ours last night,' Mary Ann told Mum. 'You can come too and meet Dad.'

'I'd like that, thank you. Soon.' She turned to me. 'Percy, I'm just going out with Ian.' This time she did name him. 'To talk somewhere neutral. Will you be all right for an hour?'

It was the first time since moving to Seggleswick that she'd asked.

'Okeydoke.' We accompanied her to the lych-gate. I was glad Mary Ann was with me.

Someone was coming down the hill, heading our way. Dr Gabriel. I started to smile at her when I heard a *crunch, crunch, crunch* of steps on the road beside us, the other side of the church wall.

Through a haze I saw a raggle-taggle bunch of boys come walking, in silence. They wore faded striped shirts over their dark breeches and had odd blue hats on their heads. A man all in black with a tall black hat led them, and their clogs hit the stone road in a raggedy march as they followed him, their eyes down. Except for one boy. Sensing me looking, he lifted his head and stared right at me. I didn't recognise him, not at first. Then he whipped off his cap and grinned. It was Morphet. His bruises were fading, he was clean, his hair was cropped. As the line went past, he waved. I grinned and waved back.

'Watch out!' Mum called as my hand made contact with skin.

'Ouch, Ben.' Liz rubbed her cheek. 'Why are you hitting me?'

I looked stupidly at my hand. 'I – I'm sorry. I didn't mean…'

Mum was talking, too. 'Ben?' she said. 'He's Percy.'

'Oh.' Liz frowned.

'Do you know each other?' Mum asked.

'Indeed we do,' she answered.

I kept quiet.

'He slept the night in our cellar.'

Mum started. 'Then it's you I have to thank! I'm his mother. Sophie. Hello.'

'Liz,' answered Liz, 'Liz Gabriel.' They shook hands.

'I am so grateful to you,' Mum said.

'A cellar?' cried Mary Ann, wide-eyed. 'Wow. When did you stay in a cellar, P?'

'Night before last,' I mumbled.

Liz stood still for a moment. 'Look, why don't you come back for tea and cake. Thomas has made some rather delicious parkin, and he'll need help eating it.'

'I'd like that very much,' said Mum, 'but may I come some other time?'

'*We* can!' Mary Ann chimed in.

Mum hesitated. 'Look, I'll see you later then, all right, love?' and she was gone.

'You did tell me that your name was Ben,' Liz reproached me when we were all seated round the table beside a glowing fire.

'He's Percy. That's why we call him P, for short,' Mary Ann told her.

'So? Which is it?' Liz asked. 'P, or Percy, or Ben?'

'Percy,' I muttered.

'So why did you say your name was Ben?'

She and Thomas and Mary Ann were all looking at me, waiting.

'Is it your second name?' she prompted.

I nodded. 'Benjamin. Then Waugh. I told you.'

Thomas barked with laughter. 'Well, my lovely. What a coincidence! Benjamin Waugh in the flesh!'

She clapped her hands. 'So, shall I call you Percy, or shall I call you Ben?'

'Ben.'

Then it happened again; I drifted sideways. We were in the same room but it was dusty and there was no furniture. Mary Ann was in her pinafore and laced-up boots, standing in front of a cupboard door beside the empty fireplace. She was beckoning me.

'What a funny-looking cupboard.' Mary Ann, in jeans, was pointing at it. 'Hey, P!' She snapped her fingers. 'Why are you looking at me like that, all woozy-like?'

I blinked hard. 'We used to go in that cupboard and explore,' I said.

Her mouth hung open. 'What?'

Liz and Thomas were looking surprised. 'He's right,' said Thomas. 'It was the entrance to a priest's hole, in the days that this place was part of the Hart's Head inn. When the inn was built, the Catholics were being persecuted but they'd meet here in the pub, secretly, with a priest. If the lookout sounded an alarm, it's where the priest could hide. And escape, get right away, too. Come, we'll show you.'

Liz led the way down the steps and round to the cellar doors and in, and on to the back where I'd slept.

'Percy knows this cellar already,' Liz told Mary Ann.

Thomas levered up the loose slab; he made it look quite easy. 'Pass us the torch.' He shone it down. A couple of steps, uneven, rough and old led downwards into darkness to where they were blocked by rubble. 'There!'

Mary Ann peered down.

'This is how the priests, and then later Jacobite rebels, could escape, if staying hidden behind the cupboard wasn't enough. The trapdoor – it would have been concealed then – led down those steps to a door on the other side. Some people say that this part may once or twice have been used as a prison.'

'Children were shut up in it as a punishment,' I said, as I stood on the edge of the hole looking down.

'Never!' Mary Ann's eyes were round.

'Were they, Ben?' Liz was watching me intently. 'What makes you think that?'

Below me I saw again a pale oval, a boy's face, with dark eyes. Tears tracked down his grubby cheeks. When he raised a hand to me, his nails and hand were black with dirt from where he'd been scrabbling to escape. As before, I took his hand and pulled. He was heavier than I'd expected, and I toppled over.

'Ow, P, that's my foot!' Mary Ann rubbed it hard.

'Did you see?' I willed her to say yes. She must have.

She looked puzzled.

Liz's eyes were trained on me. 'Why did you lose your balance, Ben?'

Would they believe me if I said?

'I think more parkin is in order,' said Liz. 'And a talk, young Ben.'

I peered into the dark openings at the side of the cellar passage as we left it, in case anyone was skulking there. But there was only us.

'Muck in, you two.' Upstairs, Thomas cut the rest of the parkin and passed it round.

'So.' Liz put her hands flat on the table. 'Ben. Let's clear up some mysteries. Is Waugh your mother's name or your father's?'

'My father's. He died.'

'And you were christened Benjamin.'

I nodded. 'After Percy, I told you. I like Ben better.' As I said it, I knew it was true.

'Me too.' Mary Ann grinned at me. I bit into the soft, sticky, treacly, gingery parkin.

'Right, Ben it is. Now. When we were in the cellar, you seemed to go, shall we say, a little strange? What was that about?'

I bit my lip.

'Did you see something?'

She might laugh at me.

'I think you may have done.'

I felt a flicker of hope; perhaps she would understand. Eyes the colour of old moss studied me and I looked back.

Mary Ann leaned forward, all excited.

I decided to trust them. 'I have funny dreams. I dream I'm in a graveyard.'

'The one here?' Mary Ann asked.

'Yes. And once, another one, like in a city. But it's not just the dreams.' Now I was hurrying to speak. 'Things happen. I've been seeing…'

'Go on.'

'Well– can you see ghosts in daylight?' I asked.

'Ah.' Liz leaned back in her chair. 'Tell me all about it, Ben Waugh.'

And I did. I left out nothing. I told them about Father and my family on the other side, about the baby and Mother dying, about the school there, about Mary Ann, about Morphet, all of it.

'Were you aware of any of this?' Liz asked Mary Ann.

Mary Ann was looking stunned. 'No. Except – he did say I was buried in the churchyard. And he comes over all funny sometimes, like just now.'

'You've never seen him in the past, or seen yourself there?'

She shook her head.

'What's your surname?'

'Spencer.'

'Spencer. I see. Mary Ann Spencer.' Liz nodded slowly. 'Am I right in thinking that there's one special grave you like to go to?' she asked me.

'The Spencer grave.'

'You see, Mary Ann, you were born the same year as Benjamin Waugh, and you lived across the square from each other. You may have been friends.'

'I don't understand.'

'No, I don't expect you do. Listen, can you come into the town centre with me? Both of you? There's something I'd like to show you.'

Thirty-eight

We almost had to run to keep up with Liz. Daniel and Harry passed us, going in the opposite direction. 'Hi, P, coming to play football?'

'Later!' I called back over my shoulder. And there, at my side, was Morphet, a spade over his shoulder, almost brushing my arm as he walked past me down the hill with other lads in their uniform. He shimmered and vanished. I stared after him then hurried after Liz and Mary Ann. Going through Kirkgate, Liz stopped so suddenly that we banged into each other like dominoes.

'Ben, where do you live in Seggleswick; is it near the graveyard?'

'A bit. It's along by the beck.' I scowled.

'Maybe for not much longer!' Mary Ann nudged me. 'My dad thinks he's found a place for you and your mum to rent. If you want it. It's near us and – Oh!'

'Really?' I stood stock-still. The world lightened. 'Where? Can we go and see it? Is your dad at home?'

'I was told not to say.' Mary Ann sounded worried. 'I don't think anything's settled. Dad and Uncle Mag want to talk to your mum first.'

'Look at you grin. Does that mean you'd like to move?' Liz asked me gently.

'Yes!'

She smiled too. 'Hold on, first things first, since we're here now. Didn't you say that you sometimes saw your ghosts in the square? Will you show us where?'

I led them to the bank on the corner.

She nodded. 'I thought so. Do you see that plaque in the wall? Well? What does it say? Read it out, go on.'

> SITE OF BIRTHPLACE
> OF THE REV. BENJAMIN WAUGH
> FOUNDER OF THE SOCIETY FOR THE
> PREVENTION OF CRUELTY TO CHILDREN
> BORN FEB. 20. 1839
> DIED MARCH 11.1908
> THE CHILDREN'S FRIEND

I'd only registered BENJAMIN WAUGH before, not the rest. Weird. But no weirder than everything else that had happened.

'He's your namesake, Ben. He was born here and he lived here when he was your age. His father was a saddler.'

'Yes, and they didn't call me Ben, they called me Benjamin. And Father... I mean, his father had a shop right here where men came with their horses.' The words came tumbling out. 'But it can't have been here. That was a big old house.'

'Correct. It was pulled down before the bank was built. Your young Ben, sorry, Benjamin, was quite a lad, "tricksy", they called him. He used to get into all sorts of scrapes. But he was brave, too. Even as a lad he stood up for others when he saw injustice.'

'Like I did... I mean, like when Benjamin stood up for Morphet.'

'That's right.'

And like I had for Harry, too, saving him from the bullies.

'Then years later, he stood up for those without a voice, after he'd become a preacher.'

Mary Ann started.

'That was after he'd moved to London. Which was also when he founded this society.'

'Against cruelty,' Mary Ann said, repeating the words from the plaque, 'like when they're abused and beaten?'

'And locked up in punishment?' I asked.

'All those, and mental cruelty too, and neglect. There are many forms, some worse than others. They can all hurt,' Liz finished.

Like not being wanted, or being shut out at night, I thought to myself. 'How do you know all this?' I asked.

'I'm a historian, as you know, and a biographer. Benjamin Waugh is who I'm writing about.'

Thirty-nine

When I look in a mirror, there's only my own reflection. I don't see the sort of other me of so long ago. Liz said that the man with a beard who appeared to me once in the bakery window and in my dreams will have been Benjamin Waugh as a grown man. She said I have piercing blue eyes like he had. Liz said I could be descended from Benjamin Waugh.

Hmm, maybe, said Mum. She doesn't know anything about my Waugh side of the family. 'There are any number of Waughs in the British Isles,' the gowk scoffed. 'Besides, Benjamin isn't even his first name, and can you imagine Percy setting up an organisation like a society for the protection of anything?'

I think he thought he was being funny.

That was when we were still with him. Things moved fast though after that. There was the wonderful day, the day when everything got better. We'd been at table, and he was mocking me for having too powerful an imagination. He said I'd been making things up, just to get attention, that I shouldn't have involved strangers in our life. I could see Mum getting annoyed. Then he said that I needed straightening out and that the discipline of a boarding school might just do that since his methods didn't seem to be effective enough. 'He can start next term,' he announced. 'It's all arranged.'

'No, Mum, I like the school I'm at!'

But I hadn't needed to say a word. It was the final straw for Mum. She was shaking her head. 'How dare you go and fix this behind my back!' she shouted. She'd never once raised her voice to him before.

The gowk's mouth opened and shut like a fish gasping for air.

I looked sideways through my eyelashes at her. 'You haven't been listening to a word I said, have you. But you're right about one thing,' she said sadly, 'Percy must leave.'

My heart sank.

'But not to boarding school. Which means I shall leave with him.'

'You can't! Where will you go?' He was pulsing deep beetroot red but was struggling to keep control. 'Did I not tell you that I would endeavour to be affectionate to the boy?'

He still didn't get it, but I did. I could feel a smile coming up me, starting at my toes.

'Yes, you did. But "endeavouring" isn't enough is it, Ian? This just proves it.' Her voice softened. 'It's too late. I'm so sorry. Listen, with the money I'll be earning from being a teaching assistant, and the savings I've got, I can afford rent for a small place.'

'But why? I don't understand.' He looked bewildered. 'You've got a perfectly good home here.'

'That's the trouble. You don't understand. This is *your* home. You've never really been able to share it, have you. We've tried, we've all tried, but it hasn't worked, has it?'

'Don't leave me!' It burst from him. His face crumpled.

A week later we'd moved out. Since then I've not seen my ghosts. But I'll never forget them. And I can only tell what I saw.

We moved to Clifford Tower at the hilly end of town, only a couple of minutes' walk away from Mary Ann and her brother and father. It's right beside the cobbled street. They're just cobbles, I know that now. From the street you come into a long room where we watch TV and use the computer, and where Mum sleeps. At the end of that room, it joins on to a tower. The tower's high up on a hillside, though you wouldn't know it from the street and the room at the front. There are two and a half small rooms in the tower, one on top of the other. At the bottom, the kitchen is just big enough for a table with two red chairs where Mum and I eat. The walls are rough and painted white and the window sills are bright red. Set flush to the wall is a barn ladder which I climb to go up to my bedroom which is just big enough for my bed and some shelves, and a bright-red windowsill, and three steps at the end of the bed to a platform with a bath on it. At night time, I can lie in the bath and watch the stars through the skylight above my head. Lying on my tummy on my bed, I'm looking out at the top branches and leaves of the tree outside, swaying and beckoning to me.

'Ben? Your friends have arrived.'

I scramble off the bed and swing down the ladder. Mum calls me Ben now, not Percy, when she remembers.

'C-come on, P.' Harry's fair dancing with impatience. He's below with Daniel and Tim and Mary Ann, who's brought Punter along. Except for Mary Ann, my friends still call me P most of the time.

'Here are your sandwiches, love. And an orange.' Mum

kisses me. 'And a chocolate flapjack and a bottle of elderflower cordial. Now off! Go!' She hugs me. 'We'll pick you up at the Falls at six, all right?'

She's coming with Mary Ann's father to pick us up. She still sees the gowk, sometimes, and on her own. But I think she likes Mary Ann's dad more.

It takes us almost an hour to walk along the river through fields of cattle where bulls, cows and calves barely bother to look up from their grazing. At our side swallows dart low over the water, hunting evening insects. We go over stiles, through squeeze-throughs, up and down, our path bending and twisting with the river, till it rises with the bank to the Falls, while the river itself is channelled into a gorge. It's not where I remember once swimming; it's bigger and wider here. By this time the sky has cleared and the sun is low and making little rainbows where it catches noisy, tumbling water as it surges down one rocky shelf of the Falls to the next to end in the deep, dark pool at the bottom. There the river is bounded by a cliff worn smooth down the centuries. We perch on rocks near the top of the Falls, on a rock shelf as close to the churning water as we can get, and take out our picnic.

Harry holds up a roll. 'Swap?' he calls, except that I can't hear him over the roar of water. I nod. Soon we're all swapping. My cheese and date sandwich for Harry's sardine and tomato roll, my tuna and cucumber for Mary Ann's damson jam. Mary Ann shares her food with Punter who wriggles in ecstasy, tail wagging.

We fall silent and carefully watch the foaming water.

I'm halfway through Harry's roll when I see them. At my

side, Daniel drops the fistful of crisps that was on its way to his mouth.

There are salmon in the bottom pool, and they're leaping.

Against the might of the water they leap. Strong and fearless. It's impossible that they can get higher. Impossible, yet they do. They jump upwards, against the pounding water, against the current. I concentrate on one fish, as long as my arm, which seems to be leading the way. It jumps up three feet, hovering in the air for the time it takes me to breathe once in and out. It falls back, the water's so strong. It thrashes in the froth and foam and tries again. Up in the air, its pink and silver scales catching the slanting sun. Back it falls.

Eight, nine, ten seconds pass.

A third time it tries. I will it on, my heart thudding. It hangs in the air, its body all muscle a-quiver. Its pink and silver scales catch the slanting sun. And then it's up and away, and flying.

What happened next to Benjamin Waugh?

Benjamin did leave Settle and go away to school. It was his uncle's school, his mother's brother, in Warwickshire, and he didn't go alone; Jane went with him and, possibly, Grace too. It was a tiny school, and Benjamin enjoyed 'five free and happy years' there. They came home in the holidays, and Benjamin's father would often go with him, rambling on the moors, exploring caves.

There is in fact very little to be found about Benjamin Waugh's childhood in Settle, but much that is in this book is based on fact. According to the census, his mother died in the same year that baby Fanny was born, and Benjamin and his sisters were then sent away to school; I cannot be sure that his mother died in childbirth, but as so many women did die then, or shortly after, it is reasonable to think that she may have done.

Eventually Benjamin became a clergyman (like his uncle) and moved to London. There, shocked by the cruelty he saw meted out to children, he set up the NSPCC for children 'of all religions and of none'. He did come back to Settle to preach, in Zion Chapel, where he'd sat as a boy, listening to other preachers. All the town came, he wrote in a letter to his daughter, whatever their religious persuasion, including the 'Nothingarians'.

Mary Ann Spencer was as real a person as Benjamin; they were the same age, and lived only a minute's walk away from each other and they may well have been friends. Mary Ann died, as on the tombstone in the book, when she was only fifteen, older though than most of her brothers and sisters. Benjamin lived into old age and died in 1908, aged sixty-nine.

Acknowledgements

My grateful thanks to Settle Public Library, to Barbara Gent and the Brayshaw Library at Giggleswick School, to St Alkeda's Church in Giggleswick, and to Bill Mitchell for granting access to archives and records. Also to Alan King for information about local tanneries, and to the Folly Museum for tips picked up during exhibitions. I am grateful to Daniel Nelson for his information on clogs, for Settle CE Primary School, their headmaster Richard Wright, and, of course, to Alex MacPherson for allowing me to be a fly on the wall; to Jean Thackeray for first showing me inside Zion Chapel and to Malcolm Bland for finding a missing gravestone needed to fill in a gap in my research. De Geus generously let me use their flat on several occasions, as did Jonathan and Cheryl their house. Helenka Fuglewicz gave encouragement at the start, and several friends read drafts of this story; Paul Clark, Ad van den Kieboom, Maydo Kooij, Carol Ann Lee, Sandy Steele and Roger Taylor gave particularly useful feedback. As did my young readers Jules Hickling and Joe Marshall. Sally Boyles generously gave of her time to copy-edit the manuscript. Chris Burgon and Lamberts Print and Design gave helpful advice throughout. The Lion and Poppies and The Talbot provided welcome writing space and good coffee and the Traddock a comfortable and friendly place to hide away.